THE SHORE OF FOREVER

the
SHORE *of*
FOREVER

ELORA MAXWELL

The Shore of Forever
Copyright © 2023 by Elora Maxwell

This novel is entirely a work of fiction. The names, characters and incidents portrayed in it are the work of the author's imagination. Any resemblance to actual persons, living or dead, events or localities is entirely coincidental.

Elora Maxwell asserts the moral right to be identified as the author of this work. Editing by Adrianne Jenks Cover art by Danna Steele

First Edition

ISBN: 979-8-37920-620-8

CHAPTER ONE

Eloisa

July 16, 1956
Bari, Italy

On our way home from shopping, Anita and I become caught up in the afternoon rush. We spent the day enjoying each other's company, and desperately trying to ignore what's to come.

"Eloisa," she says, stopping suddenly. "I'm going to miss you so much."

Turning to my dearest friend, I find the true sorrow not in her words but in her eyes.

"Do you really have to leave tomorrow? Couldn't you wait another week?" We've stopped walking altogether, and people bump into us as they try to make their way home for the night.

Pulling her out of the flow of people, I find a vacant bench and help ease her down. Anita's hands find rest on her round belly, which grows bigger by the day.

woman passes, the spell is broken, and she turns back to me, the dreamy smile of a content mother still present. "Not to mention you'll be able to study your art. You know I never had the ambition for that."

Sighing, I think of all she's lost. "Still, I feel like I need to be here for you."

"I have my Dino," she says.

Dino, her gorgeous husband would give her the world if he could. They were engaged at sixteen and married by seventeen, a year later they were expecting their first child. Now at twenty-four, they're already expecting their fourth. I love them both dearly, and I hope my marriage can be just as full of love.

Anita wipes the early onset of tears from her eyes and smiles. "We shouldn't talk of sad things today, let them wait until tomorrow." Shooting up from her spot she grabs my arm, and we continue our way down the sunny street toward my family's apartment. I lay my head on her shoulder, and she, in turn, rests hers on mine.

As we approach my home on La Bacca Street, I ready myself to walk into the flat for the last time. The home that survived so much will be but a memory tomorrow. Looking up at four stories of old bricks, some that still hold scars of the past, I suddenly feel an onslaught of emotions. Leaving Italy is very real and very scary. I come to a stop at the stairs, causing Anita to do the same. She could easily walk away and skip out on saying goodbye to my family, but she won't. She'll be here until the moment we step foot on the train.

I throw my arms around her as tightly as I can. It's difficult with her being six months along, but she returns the hug with equal strength and emotion. Without a word, we ascend the main stairs to the lobby. I can hear my younger sister upstairs, her little feet running from room to room. I smile when the stomping stops, knowing mother is scolding her.

"Come to say goodbye, Mrs. Russo?" My father's voice echoes from the door. His hat hangs low and he looks tired. Evidently, the last day at the docks has not gone as smoothly as we all wished. He has long struggled with leaving Italy, and today I assume it's hitting him harder than ever. He doesn't let Anita answer, instead, he elects to limp ahead of us and onto the stairs. It might very well be the last time he'll need to struggle to do so. I avert my gaze so he doesn't catch me looking. His injury is one of the only reminders of the war we'll take with us to America.

I can feel Anita's heavy stare on me, but I neglect it. Following my father up the stairs, I keep quiet so as not to irritate him further. His coolness toward me isn't something new, in fact, he's only gotten colder in the last few days. I know he blames me for the move we're making, I blame myself too, but I know in my heart that it's the right one.

As we enter the apartment, my mother is a bright and brilliant contrast to my father's attitude. The strongest woman I ever met, she can put dinner hot on the table while feeding my baby brother and setting the silverware. The table is set for our last dinner here.

My parents share greetings and a quick kiss before having a seat at the table. My younger sister, Lucia, runs to hug both Anita and I. Mamma grabs a chair for Anita and then takes her usual spot across from Papà. Baby Gino is slung across her chest, sleeping soundly. Anita is watching intently, just like she always does when she's over. Studying her own future.

With us all seated, we link hands for the prayer. Anita holds my right one tightly, and Lucia's little one rests in the other. Papà prays for a safe journey and gives thanks for everything the roof above our heads has given us. I wish I could say that all of my memories in the house are good ones, but I can't pretend, not even a little bit.

CHAPTER TWO

Arden

July 16, 1956
MSS Stockholm, Atlantic Ocean

The warmth from the whiskey burns my throat, shutting out the cold of the bunk room and the relentless nag of sleep that won't come. Setting the crystal glass on the dresser, I squeeze my eyes shut and gently rock back and forth over it, waiting for the images to subside. When nothing comes to me, I open my eyes and focus on the picture that rests in the corner, set in the open for all to see. Nora's eyes glare at me as if she might emerge from her chair and take the glass from my hand and toss it. Suddenly guilty, I slam the picture down and grab the half-empty glass. I step toward the rather dirty sink at the opposite wall and pour it down the drain.

The door opens and my new bunkmate Erik stumbles in. Looking at my watch, I realize that he's finished

I rest my own hands on hers to calm her. Today has come and gone far too quickly.

"Papà wants to make sure everything's in order. Plus…" I blush and dip my head and whisper, "Leo's meeting us in Naples." My voice trails off as Anita grabs my hands and squeals, her demeanor changing immediately.

"He's come to fetch you?" she asks giddily.

We'd arranged to meet my betrothed in New York, but he insisted on coming back for my family and I. He is, after all, the reason we're trekking to an entirely new country. We aren't even engaged yet, not officially anyway.

Nodding, I hold her hands in mine. "I don't know if it's all that romantic. I'm sure he just wants to make sure no one in my family gets cold feet."

"Oh nonsense, Eloisa. Anyone would be a fool to turn on the opportunity you're being granted. Besides, he loves you more than anything." Her hands go back to her round belly, and suddenly I'm ashamed.

"I am sorry that I won't be here —"

She cuts me off by pointing at the ring on her finger. "I got my happily ever after. Yours is just a little more of an adventure than mine." I almost open my mouth to protest, but she continues. "That's okay. You always were the more intrepid one of the two of us, Eloisa." She pauses a moment to watch a woman with a stroller walk in front of us, a smile crossing her face as she appears to become lost in thought. Once the on the table while feeding my baby brother and setting the silverware. The table is set for our last dinner here.

My parents share greetings and a quick kiss before having a seat at the table. My younger sister, Lucia, runs to hug both Anita and I. Mamma grabs a chair for Anita and then takes her usual spot across from Papà. Baby Gino is slung across her chest, sleeping soundly. Anita is watching intently, just like she always does when she's over. Studying her own future.

With us all seated, we link hands for the prayer. Anita holds my right one tightly, and Lucia's little one rests in the other. Papà prays for a safe journey and gives thanks for everything the roof above our heads has given us. I wish I could say that all of my memories in the house are good ones, but I can't pretend, not even a little bit.

Arden

July 16, 1956
MSS Stockholm, Atlantic Ocean

The warmth from the whiskey burns my throat, shutting out the cold of the bunk room and the relentless nag of sleep that won't come. Setting the crystal glass on the dresser, I squeeze my eyes shut and gently rock back and forth over it, waiting for the images to subside. When nothing comes to me, I open my eyes and focus on the picture that rests in the corner, set in the open for all to see. Nora's eyes glare at me as if she might emerge from her chair and take the glass from my hand and toss it. Suddenly guilty, I slam the picture down and grab the half-empty glass. I step toward the rather dirty sink at the opposite wall and pour it down the drain.

The door opens and my new bunkmate Erik stumbles in. Looking at my watch, I realize that he's finished his rounds twenty or so minutes later than he should. He softly pushes the door closed, but he jumps back upon seeing that I'm up and awake.

"I wanted to catch a last glance of home," he says, wandering to his bed and falling head first into the covers.

First day on the job, first shift; it gets to everyone. I stopped looking out for the coastline voyages ago. Every time I would look and think next time I'll retire and stay ashore. Of course that never happened, and the last time I put my feet on hard earth was nearly a year ago.

Erik's already asleep by the time I pull on my uniform jacket and slip out into the crew corridor. I have the early night shift, and I don't mind it. Most passengers are at dinner or in their cabins. Captain Nordenson should be retiring for the night in an hour or two. "103rd westbound crossing," I say to myself, checking off the number in my head. I touch the corridor wall. I've been here for all of them, and this one shouldn't be any different.

The dingy corridor gives way to the lights from a passenger hallway in the traveling class on D-deck. There are no passengers in sight, just as I suspected. I finish buttoning up my jacket by the time I get to the stairs. I brush back my hair with the comb in my pocket and decide that it's just enough to make me look presentable. I don't even need to look at my watch as I make it up to B-deck. I'm right on time to report to my superior. I check in and head out on my rounds.

As an experienced boatswain in the evening, I go about making sure all the work of the deck crew has been completed for the day. We may be a small crew, but Captain Nordenson keeps everything professional and efficient, as he has ever since he was chartering American troops to and from Europe during the war.

I start my route amongst the lifeboats now, checking to see they're all secured correctly. As I do, a crowd starts to surface from the halls below. It is a nice night out, perfect for a stroll on the decks. A family passes me by, a daughter trying to keep up with her parents who each hold a hand of hers. She's eventually swept up by her father as they continue toward the stern. I get a brief vision of my darling Klara, and then she's gone again. I turn back to my work, shutting out the pleasures of the families and couples out enjoying their evening. It's hard to push her out when I see her in everything.

"Excuse me?"

My ears perk up at the sound of a young voice. I put on the smile of a friendly crewman and turn to find two young children standing nervously in front of me. The older one, a girl, has spoken up. Crouching down to reach her eye level, I inquire as to what's wrong. "Can I help you?" I ask, keeping my hands on my knees.

The nervous girl looks at her shoes, and her younger brother reaches out to grab her hand. "We - we're lost," she says timidly.

"Well, that won't do at all now, will it?" I say. She looks up and her eyes catch the light. They're glistening with tears. Reaching out, I finally rest a hand on her upper arm. "What are your names?" I ask, my duties all but forgotten.

The girl shies away but her brother finally relinquishes. "I'm Thomas, and this is my sister Kerstin."

"Do you remember where your rooms are? Or perhaps what deck?" I ask. It is, of course, worth a shot. Every ship is a maze. Even as an experienced sailor, one can get turned around. They both shake their heads. I make sure to smile. "Well …" I say, standing. "Let's go visit my good friend, he can help us." I start to lead the children toward midship, but I'm stopped short when I feel a little hand settle into mine. Kerstin, tears still shining on her cheeks, has reached up to hold my hand. I squeeze it gently, making sure her brother is in tow before ushering them back inside.

Curt Dawe, our chief purser, resides at his desk with a book resting in his hands, though he looks disinterested in it. When he looks up, I see surprise take over his face "Lund!" he proclaims, leaning over his desk and flashing a huge smile. "What on earth have you found today?" Dawe is what you might call an entertainer. He is always interacting with the passengers, singing, or dancing around. Everyone loves him.

Reaching down I lift both kids up to let them have a seat on his desk. "Well, these two found me actually."

"Got lost did we?" he says, closing his book without marking his page. Both the kids nod, ashamed. "Hey now … there are no sour faces in this office." He swivels around in his chair and pulls the latest ship manifest from its spot on a shelf. "What are your lovely names?" he asks.

The kids look up to me as if they need my permission to interact with Dawe. I nod my head. "Kerstin. Thomas. Can you answer Mr. Dawe's question?"

"Our last name is Larsen," Kerstin says, pride inching into her voice. On cue, Dawe starts flipping through the pages. He doesn't ask any further questions, happy to have a bit of a challenge. "We're going to live in America," she says, finally smiling.

"Oh, you're on a real adventure, aren't you," I say, smiling back. She nods before looking down at her shoes, watching them swing off the edge of the table.

Turning my attention back to Dawe, I watch as he runs a finger down a page before coming to a stop in the middle. "Tourist class," he starts. "Traveling with your mother?" he asks, leaning over the large book. The kids' faces light up. Dawe looks at me in response and nods his head. "You can get back to your rounds Lund, I'll take it from here." He leans back once again and reaches for the phone to call for a female stewardess to escort the children back to their stateroom.

"Now you two," I say, crouching down once again. "You have to promise me that you'll have a great … safe voyage. No more getting lost." I cock my head and wait for an answer. They both smile and nod. "Good," I say, standing. "Mr. Dawe here is going to make sure you get back to your mother okay." As I look at Kerstin, I get a glimpse of my daughter's face again, and I have to turn away.

Returning to the deck, I start right where I left off at lifeboat six. I'll be in bed late tonight, which will certainly be putting me behind on sleep for the rest of the voyage. Tightening another slip, I try to imagine life back home, but just like everything before the war, it's fading fast. Sighing, I pull the rope even tighter and then look up at the sky, which is finally that deep shade of purple I so admire. Out here you can see every star, every twinkle of light, every possibility.

CHAPTER THREE

July 17, 1956
New York City, United States of America

Glancing up from my buttered toast, I find my husband has hidden behind his paper once again. Right on schedule. Turning to my daughters, I find them in need of no help. I watch them for a moment, envisioning them as they were when they were younger. Tearing my eyes away, I go back to my breakfast, finishing it in the silence I've become so accustomed to.

"Maman?" Juliet asks moments later.

With a smile I answer, "Yes darling?"

Martin finds the time to peer over his paper at us.

"May we be excused?" She's not even five yet, but already has impeccable manners.

Folding the napkin in my lap, I look over the girls' plates. "I want to see you each eat two more bites of your oatmeal." They scramble for their bites and push away from the table before they've even finished swallowing. I ease back as they scurry to their toys on the floor, their matching curls bouncing with each step. My heart leaps when I realize that Martin is watching just as intently. When he notices me watching him he goes back to his reading, and I back to pretending that nothing's off between us.

We haven't spoken, truly spoken to one another, since we were home. When we left Paris to come visit my family here in the States, old wounds opened, and we let them fester. It didn't help that a few old flames came to call upon me, or that my parents still didn't understand the path I chose in life. It's not either of our faults that we ended up together, that would be God's, and he doesn't make mistakes.

I leave the table and walk to the window that overlooks the New York City harbor. Out of the corner of my eye, I watch my girls play with their dolls on the floor. I love my life. America or France, it doesn't really matter as long as I have them. Martin comes to join me a minute later. He kisses me atop my head and wraps an arm around my waist, but I can't help but wonder if it's a front, more play-acting.

"I am sorry that we have to go so soon," he says, holding me close. I let my guard down and fall into him. Although I wish he'd relayed his sympathies when we were leaving my actual home, I appreciate that he's trying now.

"We'll just have to come back and visit soon," I say, trying to keep the bitterness from my voice. The last time I'd seen home, seen my family before this trip, was four years ago. Johanna and Juliet were only ten months old then.

"We will," he says. He kisses me again, only to leave my side for his coat and the door. "I figure, being in New York, I would get some business done, *non?*" He flashes his boyish smile, and I find myself giving a half-hearted one in return. He leaves without so much as a goodbye.

In a fit of skirts, I collapse onto the couch. My thoughts wander to the business, our marriage, and the transatlantic crossing that awaits us. My notions are soon interrupted by two little bodies clambering up to sit beside me, both insisting I look at the outfits they've chosen for their dolls today.

The television and the girls keep me occupied throughout the rest of my morning. We have lunch in the hotel restaurant and go for a walk around the pool and garden. It's hot and sunny out, something that I have dearly missed during my time in Paris. I let the sun drench me in warmth, imagining that I'm back home on my family's farm on a humid July day. Johanna tugs on my arm, and I emerge back to the landscape of a tiny hotel courtyard, my two young girls peering up at me. I smile sweetly at them before we continue our stroll. Other mothers walk the paths with their children, husbands undoubtedly out on business or in the hotel café. It does little to comfort me in my feelings of loneliness.

"Maman?" Juliet asks, twirling around to face me.

"Yes, darling?" I reply, reaching out to smooth her hair.

"I'm hot," she whines, pulling away from my touch.

The girls have been chasing each other around in circles and singing, "Alouette, Gentille Alouette". I smile, proud of the color in her cheeks. In the past two weeks, the girls have become accustomed to, and even welcoming of, the outdoors. To see them pet a cow, gather eggs, and play fetch with the puppies made the trip worth it for me. I know it made my parents happy to see their grandbabies running around the land they worked so hard to cultivate. I felt myself coming back down to earth too, trading my curls for braids and my skirts for my old overalls.

"Maman!" Juliet whines, pulling away.

"Sorry, Juliet," I say, coming back to reality. "Let's go get some ice cream." The girls' faces ignite with smiles as they jump up and down. I grab both their little hands and we skip toward the lobby.

Lucky for us there's a parlor right down the street. Although big buildings surround it and cars beep as they buzz by, for a moment, the exterior reminds me of the one on the main street back home. But inside it's modern and not at all like the one back home. My illusion once again fades, leaving heartache in its wake. My girls have already climbed up on individual stools and begun to pester the soda jerk.

"I'll take a Coke," I say, having a seat in between the girls. I place a few coins down on the table and let him go to work. "I'll Be Home" is playing on the juke-box, what wouldn't I do for some Kitty Wells or Hank Snow right now. Suddenly, my heart is aching again, I know I won't be hearing much American music when I return to France. It's enough to make me cry.

Hearing slurping beside me, I look and see Johanna has dripped chocolate ice cream down her chin and all over her blue dress. I grab a few napkins and go to work cleaning her up the best that I can.

The television is the only light in the loft. The girls are bathed, fed, and now rest comfortably in their beds. I have just put my rollers in and am adorned in my robe and pajamas. It's not that late, at least not late enough to feel worried or angry. Looking out at the harbor, I see ships coming and going, individual cities on the water. I swallow the fact that I'm leaving America again. I've done it before, but this is the first time I truly don't want to. During the war, I did it to serve my country. When I ran away with Martin, it was for the adventure. This time is harder, nearly impossible.

The front door creaks open and Martin pads inside. I give him a forced smile, and he gives one in return. Meeting him in the kitchen, I rest my hands on the back of a chair, waiting for him to speak. He bypasses me and takes a seat on the couch. I let out an impatient breath and follow him. I don't sit with him, instead, I stand behind him. I rest one hand on his shoulder, and to my surprise, he reaches back for it and brings my knuckles to his lips.

"How was your day, *ma chérie*?" he asks, turning to me.

My heart flutters to life. Rounding the couch, I have a seat next to him and lay against his chest, hoping his need for conversation will outlast the commercial break.

CHAPTER FOUR

Eloisa

November 12, 1948
Bari, Italy

Yesterday was my sixteenth birthday. It was a happy affair, even though my mother is due to have a baby any day now, and my father has not smiled these last few months. Despite everything, she still found the time to bake me a lemon cake, and he found the money and the joy to give me a gift and a brief smile.

The parcel was neatly wrapped in a brown paper bag and tied with string from an old dress of mine, but its contents were more valuable to me than gold: a dozen freshly sharpened colored pencils neatly packed together, and five new sketchbooks of varying sizes laid in wait for me to use them.

Of course, the special day gave way to night, and then today dawned and my parents were back to their normal selves — Mamma slaving away in the house and

Papà returning to the docks to work. I do what I can for Mamma around the house, but as she tucks herself away in bed for a nap, I take to the street to find something worth breaking in my new pencils. Sitting down on a bench across from my house, it's not long before something worthy of drawing stumbles upon me.

Leo Marino, a boy I could never truly forget, staggers by while looking up at the windows of my family flat. I freeze. I'm surprised to be seeing him at all, let alone in front of my home. I watch as he reaches down to the street and finds a pebble. He weighs it in his hand, bouncing it in his palm before winding up to throw it.

Not wanting him to disturb my mother, I jump from my perch, knocking my new pencils from my lap as I launch myself at him, catching his wrist before he can expel the rock. When he turns to look at me, shock runs through his face before recognition dawns.

"You're here!" he exclaims.

"You're here," I echo back. I can hardly believe it. The boy that left me two years ago to follow his family across the world has returned to me. And he's smiling.

He pulls me in for a hug, and the first thing I notice is how good he smells. Not wanting to question things yet, I pull him in tighter and latch my arms around him. His letters had been consistent throughout our time apart, but never once did he mention coming back to visit. I reluctantly pull away to get a better look at him. He's taller, but the Leo I knew is still prevalent in his facial features and in the way he carries himself.

"You're probably wondering what I'm doing here," he says, rubbing the back of his neck.

"I don't know what I'm wondering," I laugh. This is all too magical; it has to be a dream.

The right side of his mouth curls into a smile before he shyly looks down. "I just missed you."

My heart flutters in my chest, but then my head catches up and I realize it hardly makes sense. "How on earth did you manage this?"

"Caught a ship out of New York." He shrugs as if it's no big deal.

"It must've cost a fortune."

He looks me up and down. "Well worth any amount of money to see you."

I blush, initially, before widening my eyes, willing him to expose the truth.

"All right, all right," he says, holding his hands up. "You caught me. I know your birthday was yesterday, so I figured I'd take you to the movies."

I peer up at the apartment. "I would love that Leo, I really would, but I can't be that far from my mamma for too long. She's due any day now."

"Isn't your papà around?"

I force a smile. "Oh, you know him, working."

He puts his hands on his hips and glances around, settling on the mess I've made by the bench. He points at it and walks over, bending to pick up the pencils that had been scattered. "Still drawing?" he asks.

"Yeah," I say, not trying to sound too excited about it.

"You never send me anything," he teases. He settles on the bench and begins to flip through the empty pages.

I reach out to stop him before he gets too far. "I just got that yesterday." Sitting next to him in a huff, I pull the book from his grasp and wrap my arms around it, locking it to my chest. "Listen, you better tell me why you're really here."

"All right fine," he relents. "I was sent by my mother to visit my uncle and escort one of my little cousins to America."

The news of someone leaving would have shocked me a year ago, but now it's expected. "You came at the right time then," I say, solemnly.

He reaches out and rests his hand on my exposed wrist. "Have things gotten worse for your family?"

I shake my head. "It's not that they've gotten worse. They just haven't gotten better. Everyone is either sick or sad."

"You know my offer still stands." Leo caresses my hand now.

"And you know my papà would never agree to it."

"Lots of girls your age are going. There's work for you there, you can make your own way in the world," he explains.

I roll my eyes and shake my head. "Have you met Marco and Carlotta Nicoletti?" My parents would never allow it.

"Yes, the most traditional Italians I've ever met. But Eloisa, you would be happy there. I know it."

The thought had crossed my mind in recent months. We had always been the family that stick up their noses and judged those who left the country behind, but if we aren't happy here, then I don't see a reason to stay.

"I'd do anything to go with you," I blurt out.

"I'd take you with me if I could."

Suddenly his hand is on my cheek and he's brushing the hair from my face. He doesn't go further than that, doesn't kiss me or pull me forcefully to him, he just looks into my eyes.

"How long are you in town?" I whisper.

Realizing we're in the open street, he pulls away to answer. "Only two days."

"Two days and you're spending some of it with me?" I breathe. My voice catches, and I'm filled with excitement at the thought. I haven't felt like a priority lately, but Leo's offer changes all of that.

"And I'll be back tomorrow," he says, reaching out to touch my cheek again, but he stops himself before his fingers have a chance to brush against my skin. "I just have to eat dinner with my family tonight, the rest of the time I want to spend with you."

"Dinner?" The sun is already on its journey down, signifying the late hour. "Your family lives on the other side of town. You'll be late.

"I know," he flashes a mischievous grin.

His eyes haven't left mine, and I'm fighting hard to find a reason to keep him here with me. Reluctantly, logic wins out and I have to push him away. "You should go see your family, and I should go tend to mine."

"Fine, you win this time, but I'll be back tomorrow." He pushes himself up from the bench and lends me an arm. We don't know how to say farewell, so we settle for a quick hug and an awkward wave.

How am I so unlucky that must I go through life without him? I hate the idea that we are destined to continue to meet this way, like ships passing in the night. I don't want to live life without him beside me, and yet, I feel that I will.

CHAPTER FIVE

Eloisa

July 17, 1956
Naples, Italy

This is officially the furthest from home I've ever been. Every step from this point forward is into the unknown. My eyes are glued to the window, my fingers frozen to my pencil. I'd been drawing, but with everything outside the window so new and incredible, I can't bring myself to look back down at the paper.

The little ones are asleep, Gino in mother's arms and Lucia curled next to me. My father reads the paper, while my mother is as equally intrigued as I. The more I look at her the more the intrigue turns to nerves — nerves that she'd never let on about.

Tucking my legs and skirt underneath me, I flip the page and begin drawing my mother how she is, soft yet strong. Her eyes are moist, but she holds Gino close to her with an unyielding grip. I glance at my

"You and Leo run along," she says, stacking two bags and lifting at the knees. With Gino on her opposite hip, she balances the cases on her free one. Looking back at me she winks. "Go. We'll meet you at our hotel after dinner."

I reach forward again, determined to help, but also determined to have time to freshen up. "Mamma let me —"

"I won't hear it." She gestures her head toward the town. "Go enjoy your evening. You both deserve to catch up without the rest of us listening in."

My father doesn't say a word, instead he shifts his eyes to Leo, who nods and reaches for my hand.

"I know just the place." Leo tugs me gently. "It's not far, I promise."

I reluctantly turn away from my family and take to his side. I hold tight to the arm he extends and move with him. Once we're a block away, I dare to open my mouth. "Well, you weren't much help just then, were you?" I say with a laugh.

"How could I disobey an order from Mrs. Nicoletti?" he says with a shrug. "Am I to believe you wanted to bypass a little evening with me?" he teases.

I stop. "That wasn't it at all," I stammer. "I simply wanted to change into something a little more appealing." I search his eyes for a moment for something different, but they're the same as they have been since he was a child, all shiny and filled to the brim with tenderness.

He gently grabs my forearm, shaking me slightly. "Eloisa, you're beautiful."

I let a smile erupt across my face and stretch on my tiptoes to plant a kiss on his lips. He goes to reel me in, but I fall back onto my heels, and with a laugh, start to lead him away. He's left frozen with a grin on his own face. "Come on," I giggle. "I'll sneak another one after you take me to dinner. I'm famished." With the swing of my purse and a little skip, I put a few paces between us. He hurries to catch up. Putting his hand in mine, he swings it to match my giddiness.

"Well, we better hurry to dinner then," he says. I lean into him as we make our way down the sidewalk, arm in arm.

We have our meal at a lively spot in town. Just as Leo said, the restaurant is only two blocks away from the station. The *aperitivi* and *antipasti* are accompanied by polite conversations and gentle inquiries about life. I tell him about Anita and her growing baby, and how much the town has changed since he last visited. I tell him about the journey from home and little Gino. He reciprocates with tales of his own. I hang on to every word that spills from his mouth about America. Every detail helps me to imagine how my new home will look, how it will feel, and how it will simply be.

"I can't wait to take you to Coney Island," he says, popping the final ravioli from his fork and into his mouth. "Your drawings will be spectacular." He pauses a moment. "I keep telling my friends that they won't need a camera for long 'cause my girl has an eye for detail, unlike any Kodak."

"Oh, I don't know about that Leo." I laugh and push my plate back, making room for my sketchbook. Digging into my handbag, I pull it out and open it to one of my more recent pieces. Anita stands at a railing overlooking the harbor. Leo turns it toward him, and I see the emotion switch behind his eyes. I feel a sudden urge to defend myself. "We went all throughout town that final week, so I could remember it how I wanted to." I take an anxious sip of water as he flips through the pages, pulling it closer.

"Is it —" He looks up at me, letting the book fall flat on the table. "Is it back to how it was before?"

"The harbor?" I ask.

"All of it."

I think of my answer carefully. There'd been wonders done since the end of the war, but she still holds scars, we all do. "For the most part." I think of my father and our little brick building on La Bacca, how the people still look up at the sky late at night out of fear of what the dark might hold. "It's hard to move on when there's so few left to bear the burden." I hadn't meant it as a way to blame him, if I had, it would put me in that same boat.

"Eloisa, you know that we had to leave when we did."

Reaching across the table I grab his hands. I'd long since forgiven him and his family. They'd made it through the war and suffered through the disasters like the rest of us. "I know you did." I smile slightly before pulling my hands away.

After our shared silence, Leo signals to the waiter for the bill. Once the man returns, Leo takes his wallet from his back pocket and counts the bills. I pretend to be occupied with reaching for my sketchbook as I peek over his hands and see that his wallet is overflowing with cash. I immediately avert my eyes. I only dare to look back up when he reaches out a hand to help me up from the table. I smile again and take it. I hang my bag on my opposite shoulder and hook my free hand through his arm.

We wander outside into the brilliance of the dying day, the streets softly illuminated by the *lampioni* and storefronts that line them. Accompanied on the side-walks by a few other couples, we head back toward the hotel.

A street performer plays his guitar and sings in Italian, an older tune, something I remember my mother singing to me years ago. Leo leads me to a bench a few feet away. A crowd has gathered, but we still have a clear view of the man. It's only now that I realize he is blind. Leaning forward, I try to imagine a story for him. Born with it? War wound perhaps?

"Aren't you going to draw him?" Leo asks.

I look between Leo's sparkling gaze and the misty eyes of the blind man. I realize that I don't want to draw him.

"I want to draw you," I let out.

He gives me a smirk and sits up straighter, looking at me head-on.

Embarrassed to say more, I take out my book and go straight to work. I'm able to avoid his eyes until I get to his face. I should be able to draw it from memory, but I can't. My hands stall and I'm forced to look at him. We've both changed, that much is clear, but I still love him more than anything. The pencil rolls from my hand, stopping itself in the center crease of my book. I reach out to him, and he does the same. His hand rests on my cheek and we huddle closer together. We share a sweet kiss and a smile.

The streets are nearly empty when we finally make our way to the hotel, the lights from the *lampioni* causing the diamond on my hand to shimmer. He'd told me months ago that the ring had been lost in the mail. I'd thought maybe he'd changed his mind, that it was an easy way to save me some embarrassment. But no. He'd simply wanted to give it to me in person. I smile and grip his hand a little tighter. After a year of him posing the question via a letter, I'd been able to tell him *yes* in person. The ring made the engagement feel official.

At the hotel, we share one last kiss in the lobby, this one causing my stomach to do somersaults. The pressure of his lips lingers on mine as he kisses my knuckles and turns away. The elation turns to panic as I head to the front desk to collect my room key. What would my parents say? They'd blessed the match months ago, naturally, but what would they say now that we've officially left home and are headed across the ocean to start a new life?

Luckily, I'm spared the firestorm of attention because, when I sneak in, I find the entire family asleep. Moving to the bathroom, I slip inside with my bag and turn on the light. Looking in the mirror, I notice my face is flushed, and my lower lip is still swollen from the kiss we shared downstairs. Brushing my finger across it, a chill runs through me.

How grown up I look. Standing a little straighter, the gawkiness, and the softness, of my youth disappears before my very eyes. What once was uncertainty has been replaced with confidence. More change. My newfound confidence falters and, swallowing the sudden wave of nerves, I splash water on my face and begin to wash the makeup from it. I roll up my hair and change into my pajamas.

I've become the person I've wanted to be for so long ... his fiancée.

CHAPTER SIX

Arden

July 17, 1956
MS Stockholm, Atlantic Ocean

D ays like today are why I continue to sail. Calm days when I can keep to myself and keep my mind at peace. Not like how it was during the war or even before it. Then I'd had something waiting for me at home, I had a greater purpose. Now I know nothing but sailing. I don't have to focus on anything but my daily routine. At fifty years old, there's nothing I'd rather be doing than sailing on this ship. At 525 feet and a tonnage of 12,165, the Stockholm is the smallest ship on the North Atlantic route. She may be small, but she is the pride and joy of Sweden — the closest I can bear to being home.

I look up from winding my watch as I enter the main dining room. Glorious Kurt Jungstedt paintings adorn the walls, an homage to her homeland. I hurry on, not wanting passengers to notice me. A cool breeze meets me as I emerge onto the boat deck. The sun is just now starting to sink. I should be sleeping before my late shift, but the ocean is tranquil, and the sky is clear.

"Taking in the day Lund?"

I know the voice before I even turn around. "Captain Nordenson, sir," I say with a salute.

Harry Gunnar Nordenson is the kind of man that you don't find yourself in a room with too often. He is contemplative and hard to read at times; a man who doesn't take too much time out of his day to talk about trivial things.

"Enjoy the easy night, you never know what this July weather has in store." He tips his hat and heads toward the captain's quarters.

I nod my head at his back and turn out toward the water. It was unusually cool for the day, which might make for nasty fog at some point.

Once I've had enough of the view, I slink back inside. Through the labyrinth, I descend into the mess hall. I've managed to miss the rush of the evening shift's lunch break, something I learned to achieve very early on in my career. In fact, it's such an odd time that only Evert Svensson mans the kitchen.

"Hey, Arden!" He says from behind the stove. "I was just about to take my lunch break. There's some leftover soup."

her lap. It's the scene that sits on my dresser, the last clear picture I have left of them, the last good memory I seem to remember. I'd taken the photo from the front lawn on a camera we had borrowed from a neighbor. Of course, we had the family photo taken next, but it turned to ash in London during the blitz, along with most of everything else.

London, that infernal city.

I reach my doorstep as my thoughts turn toward our life in London. I know what's to come, and it's usually debilitating. I calmly unlock my door and shuffle to my nightstand, fumbling with the drawer. Even with my shaky hands, I manage to pull out a glass and a half-empty whiskey bottle. I pour a glass just as my mind takes me to the Stockholm docks, where we first embarked on our journey to new lives in England. The hot liquid reaches my lips just as the final scene forms in my head. I was at the pub, just down the road from our flat when the first bombs were dropped. I take another long draw, focusing on the burn in my throat. The whiskey does its normal trick of numbing everything, including my thoughts. I let out a long exhale, having staved off the worst of it.

Even though it's dark, I can still sense my wife's heavy gaze on me from the photo on the dresser. I turn to the bottle, ashamed. I start to pour a third but realize that if I don't stop now, I won't have enough to last the final days of the voyage. I make a mental note to ask Lucas to sneak me an extra bottle once we arrive at port for the trip back. Slipping my liquid therapy back into its place, I take my jacket off and sling it across the banister. I stand there a moment contemplating the sudden fuzziness of my vision, before finally falling face-first into bed for a quick nap before my evening rounds.

CHAPTER SEVEN

Adeline

December 9, 1944
Nancy, France

My tired eyes haven't been closed for more than three seconds before the tent flap is pulled back and light floods in. A collective groan rises up from the girls around me. "We have men trickling in from the fighting near Lorraine. Captain Hill wants all hands on deck," came the exhausted voice of Claire, one of my many roommates. A few women get up without complaint, most of whom have had a decent rest since their last shift.

"Do you want the night shift out there too?" Marilyn calls from a few beds down.

"Captain Hill's orders!" Claire calls, making her way into our tent.

I pull my wool blanket over my head for just a moment before hopping out of bed with the rest of the stragglers. When I get outside, I realize it's not as bad as it was made out to be. Many of them are walking, which is good. I was expecting stretchers upon stretchers, something close to how it had been when we first landed in August.

Caught doing nothing, Captain Lillian Carter approaches me. "Adeline, go look after the men in the first-floor ward with Julia and Annette." I take a breath and salute her even though she's already passed by.

Annette is already dressing wounds when I enter, while Julia is sitting on a stool next to a cot, leaning close to the man that resides there.

"Adeline," Julia waves me over. "Can you sit here with him?" I look down at the man and see that his eyes are darting back and forth, and he's mumbling.

"What has happened to him?" I ask, reaching down and placing a light hand on his shoulder.

"They stitched a severe cut at the base of his skull before sending him in here. He's mumbling in French."

I stand up a little straighter. Even though my French is shaky at best, the girls still made me their resident translator. "Isn't there something more important for me to do?" I ask, rubbing my temples to stave off the sleepiness that has stalked me since getting out of bed. There's little I can do for a man who is barely conscious.

"Listening to this man is important," Julia says. She is the most compassionate in the group by far. She's only a year younger, but already has more experience than me, and far more empathy. "You had a rough shift yesterday; you could use the break," she says, her voice lowering to a whisper. I flinch at the fact that she noticed my long line of bad luck with patients the day before. Julia rests her hand on my arm. "Just comfort him, he's the only Frenchman here as far as I can tell." Seeing my disappointment she whispers, "I'll call you if there's anything else."

She leaves me to attend to the next patient, bending over the soldier one cot over. Sighing, I sit on the stool she left and stare at the man. Putting my elbows on my knees I lean forward and rest my chin in my hands. His eyes open when I put two fingers on his throat.

"I'm just checking your pulse soldier." His eyes aren't as manic as they were moments before, but they seem to have settled on me. His lips move with a mumble. I lean over, my ear centimeters from his mouth.

"*S'il te plaît, peux-tu me tenir la main et prier avec moi*," he whispers. Something about prayer and something else about my hand. He says it louder, "*Peux-tu me tenir la main et prier avec moi, s'il te plaît?* His eyes start to dart around the room once more, his hand grasping for something that isn't there. My heart breaks for him.

"Miss?" I turn to a young British soldier whose arm is in a sling across his chest. "He wants you to hold his hand and pray with him." I immediately find the soldier's hand and hold it tight. He stops flailing around but the whispers continue.

"Do you know this man?" I ask the Brit, who's now sitting on an empty cot.

"No miss, I'm afraid I don't. I saw him on the road here, I think, but he was out cold then."

"Thank you." I turn back to the Frenchman. "I'm afraid I don't know many prayers," I say in English. He calms at the sound of my voice, so I continue to talk. Soon his eyes close and he drifts off to sleep. I gently lay his hand on his chest. When I stand, I realize just how tired I am. I nearly fall back down on the little stool, but when I look to my left, I see a soldier trying and struggling to stand.

There is no rest for the weary. Not for him, not for me.

When I reach him, the young man is frustrated. "Can I help you, soldier?" Annette joins me before he can answer.

"Ben, the surgeon said you shouldn't be up and about." She takes his arm and eases him back. The boy's eyes are filled with tears.

I crouch down next to him. "Do you have any pain?" I ask, trying to get him to calm.

"My brother is in surgery," he says. I look up at Annette and swallow hard, cases like these rarely end happily. "He was pretty bad off when we came in ..." he trails off.

"We can't have you up and about," Annette says, propping his bandaged leg up on a folded blanket. As he starts to protest, Dr. Zinschlag enters the room.

When he spies Annette and me, my head immediately drops. Dr. Zinschlag's own brother had been lost on D-Day. When he came into the patient wards it often meant he was on a tour of telling brothers and friends that their loved one had been lost.

"I'm looking for Benjamin Wright," he whispers, resting a gentle hand on Annette's shoulder. I squeeze my eyes shut and turn away; I simply can't take hearing more bad news. I'm a few steps away when I hear Benjamin begin wailing. Hearing a man cry is something I'll never quite get used to.

I run into Julia, "What's going on? Who's hurt?" I step aside, and she goes rigid when she sees Dr. Zinschlag. "Can't he find another way to go about telling the poor lads?"

"It's how he stomachs the guilt." A chill runs through me as I imagine having someone in my care die on my watch.

Someone calls for a nurse across the room. Julia leaves me with a sad smile and a reassuring squeeze. I turn my own thoughts back to the men in my row. They seem at peace for the moment, most sleeping soundly after having found a relatively safe place. Rubbing my eyes in defense against an oncoming headache, I figure now would be a good time to clock out. If I could just get a few hours of sleep before my night shift, I would be reinvigorated. With the wave of injured men officially diminished, I check on each of my patients one last time. I stop at the Frenchman who is now awake. Just from looking at him, I can tell that he's calmer.

"Can I have some water?" he asks in a breathtakingly thick accent. His sudden English surprises me. Reaching for a pitcher, I pour some into a tin and hold it to his lips. I slowly tip it so he doesn't aspirate on it; he gulps until it's gone. I set the cup down and hover over him.

"Is there anything else that you need?" I ask gently.

"Can you tell me where I am?" he asks calmly.

"You're currently with the 12th at our evacuation hospital in Nancy. As far as I know, you came from a battle near Lorraine. I'm sorry, I don't know more than that." I watch as he tenses up and then starts to shake, I've seen the tremors in other men before. They're calling it a combat stress reaction or shell shock. Kneeling beside him quickly I grab his hand and start speaking to him. "What's your name, soldier?"

"Martin Darbonne."

I squeeze his hand harder as the tremors ravage on. Keeping his focus on me, I introduce myself. "Martin, I'm Adeline. I'm a nurse, and I'm going to take care of you." He nods. "Just keep breathing, okay?" With my free hand, I brush his hair to the side. For the first time, I can clearly see his hazel eyes; they take my breath away.

CHAPTER EIGHT

Adeline

July 17, 1956
New York City, United States of America

It seems that Martin has arranged a little family outing for us this fine July day. He tells us it's a surprise, but I know the moment we cross into Brooklyn that we're headed for Coney Island. I'm honestly surprised at his sudden urge to spend a day with us. He's only shared a few words with me the past few days, being so caught up in work and all. I bristle at the thought of him needing to butter me up before he drops something on me, but I shake it off. My husband wouldn't sink so low as to bribe me.

He offers me his hand with his fingers outstretched, so I unfold my arms and let him take the lead. I turn to my girls and smile. They're sitting on their knees looking out the bus window, watching their world slowly open to them. The skyscrapers are beginning to give way to shops and boardwalks. The girls show true excitement when the roller coaster appears. The ride that adorns postcards and knick-knacks would inevitably make me sick, should I take a spin on it.

"Papa! What is this place?" Johanna asks.

He leans in close to the girls. "A magical place they call Coney Island."

Their little mouths drop open, and they go back to looking out the window. I smile genuinely and look over at my husband, who in turn is looking at me lovingly. I squeeze his hand as the bus comes to a stop.

We each take a girl's hand and exit into the bright sunlight. I take my sunglasses from my bag and put them on. The twins are wearing their bright blue sun dresses and look as if they're ready to take on the world. Juliet pulls me forward and we're off.

For the first hour or so, the girls insist on trying every stand on the strip. We eat hot dogs, play games, and ride the rides. We watch the girls ride ponies and get fooled by a magician who pulls coins from their ears. There's a new ride that goes through a dark tunnel. The girls take the car in front of us, while Martin and I sit behind them. I thread my arm through his and lay my head on his shoulder. In response, he leans over and kisses me on the head. The ride is full of silly scenes and paints that glow.

Meeting up with the girls on the other side, we walk back out onto the midway, at which point Johanna complains that her feet hurt. Martin scoops her up and puts her on his shoulders. Upon seeing the special treatment, Juliet does the same.

"Come on darling," I say, crouching down. I can't lift her to my shoulders, but she is able to climb onto my back. Martin lends me a hand and the four of us go on our way again.

The sun has started to sink a little lower, casting the large shadow of the roller coaster across us.

"What will it take to get you to ride that?" Martin asks.

I scoff at the proposition. "There's not enough money in the world."

"Oh, come on Adeline. You've jumped out of a plane before, there's no way it's worse than that."

As if on cue, the coaster cars come zooming by and are accompanied by terrified screams. "That was one time." I hardly want to remember that moment in my life, but the experience, like the entirety of the war, has made me who I am today. I squint into the sun, looking up at the monster. It isn't that tall. I'd conquered far more in life so far, what was this wooden scream machine?

"Come on Maman!" Juliet says from my back.

"Yes, come on Maman," Martin says, looking extremely hopeful.

"We'll cheer you on," Johanna offers.

I take a deep breath and then start walking toward the entrance. A series of cheers and claps from Johanna and Martin follows me.

The wait is agonizing. When we get to the loading platform, Martin steers me to the very front. I groan in annoyance. I suppose I'll be facing it head-on then. The girls cross over to the exit and wait by the gate, their little eyes just visible over the top. I picture them standing on their tippy-toes and I smile.

The restraints are checked and then the car is in motion. At first, I squeeze my eyes shut and grasp for Martin's arm. But as the lift hill clicks, I realize I want to experience it all, even if I'm scared. When I open my eyes, I'm given a beautiful view of the city in one direction and the sea in the other. There's a cacophony of delighted screams, mine included. The drop, paired with the tight twists and turns, is exhilarating; a sense of adventure I haven't felt since the day I got married. When we pull back into the loading station, Martin and I are beaming and laughing with delight. He escorts me from our seats and leads me over to the girls, who are staring intently. Before we've even exited, they swarm us with their questions.

"Maman, please bring us back here when we're old enough to ride!" Juliet says, watching the next train ascending the hill.

"Tomorrow?" I ask Martin.

He grins. "Someday," he says in response.

To end our excursion, we find a little spot on the beach. While still busy for that time of day, there's plenty of space for our little family. Smoothing my skirt underneath me, I plop down onto the sand. Martin and the girls drop their shoes by me and race to the water. Laughter fills the air as the girls chase the waves in and out. Martin occasionally attempts to splash them when they're not expecting it, causing a fun game of tag.

There's no doubt that the water's chilly. Having no desire to be cold, I use the time to take it all in. Pulling my skirt taut, I sit back on the sand, still warm from a long day in the sun, and dig my hands into it. Looking up at the puffy white clouds in the sky, I close my eyes, taking in all the sounds and smells. Perfection never lasts in my experience, but perhaps it doesn't need to last all that long in order to appreciate it. I've learned to grasp on to days like today, to hold them tight. Opening my eyes back up to the world around me, I see that the girls have started to splash back at their father.

"Do you need reinforcement darling?" I call out to the poor outnumbered man.

I've distracted him just long enough for the girls to douse him in water. Completely proud of my girls and their cleverness, I hop to my feet and jog toward them, stopping just short of the water line where the three of them stare at me and contemplate whose team I'll join. Keeping my expressions neutral, I crouch down and let the water run into my palms. Quicker than lightning, I burst up and toss my meager contribution at Martin's chest, which is already soaked.

I squeal and make a run for it, but he catches me and drags me back to him. I lose my footing and fall straight back into the water. No use in playing it safe now that I'm drenched. On my cue, the girls rush forward and tackle their father. Soon we're all drenched head to toe, happy and laughing. I catch a glimpse of Martin smiling, really smiling. I pause a moment and smile back at him.

Perfection.

The girls fell right to sleep on the bus ride home. Filled with hot dogs, cotton candy, and a new treat called funnel cake, they crashed from the sugar as soon as they sat down. Juliet lays her head on my lap, and I run my fingers through her hair as she sleeps. Martin has a hand on Johanna's back as she dozes on and off.

"Thank you for this, Martin," I say, laying my head against his shoulder.

"I know it's been rather tough on you girls." I squeeze my eyes shut, trying not to think of the circumstances.

"It has," I say, my heart skipping a beat upon realizing that he has been paying attention to how I've suffered over the past few days.

He leans down and kisses me on the head. "I love these girls, Adeline. I love you too, please know that. You are my world."

I sit up, wanting to see the love in his eyes. I hold my hand to his cheek. "I love you too, Martin." It's true, what I've said, I've loved him since the day I met him.

As the bus continues to jolt along, I hold tightly to my husband's arm, content in pretending we're not sitting in a box with strangers. Let them stare. A lot of people have moved on from the romanticism of the 40s, but I refuse to. Why should I want to trade in the passion I experienced for the cookie-cutter life everyone is so desperate to have these days? Looking around me, I see a combination of both. We seem so out of place with our sandy, saltwater-stained clothes. We're a perfectly normal family with our two daughters wedged between us, sleeping after a long day, and yet, my husband's arm is draped around me protectively. I notice there's no sort of affection between the couples around us.

When I catch Martin's eye, I can see how alert he still is, even after an adventurous day, the same alert eyes accompanied by the face I've come to memorize. I suppose we're both still trying to find a balance. A balance between our past life as trailblazing adventurers and our new one as partners in raising our beautiful daughters amidst the outrageously rigid rules of our world.

CHAPTER NINE

Eloisa

July 18, 1956
Naples, Italy

I suppose today's the day I'll be leaving Italy for good. In a few short hours, I'll have nothing ahead of me but the ocean and a future in America. Seeing as this is a momentous occasion, I've chosen my most stylish outfit for the day. It's a brilliant rose-red dress with a volumized skirt that's fitted at the waist. Anita had picked it out for me months ago for this exact moment.

For a second, I can almost envision her next to me in her matching dress, baby in her arms, ready to take on the world with me. Her whole family will join us someday, but until then, I need to focus on the things I have. Trying to push Anita from my head, I twist the base of my lipstick and finish off the look. Taking one more glance in the mirror on my way out the door, I think I just might look attractive. I toss my handbag over my shoulder and skip through the hotel with a smile on my face.

My confidence dissipates when I reach *il caffè*. I'm awkward with my hands, and not sure what to do about the ring. I hide it behind my back at first, but I haven't gotten used to the feel of it yet, so I end up fidgeting with it. I'm trying not to make it so obvious, but when I see Leo, I let my hands drop, the diamond shimmers in the natural morning light leaking into the room.

My mother sees it first and rises to greet me. She throws her arms around my neck and holds my face, before taking my fingers in her hands to study the ring. "It's absolutely stunning Leo." She turns to Leo and my father with the biggest smile, a smile that drains the dread and anxiety from my body.

My younger sister approaches me and beams at the ring, her head surely taking her off on a fairy tale journey. My father hardly seems affected. He raises his glass to us, and with a nod, goes about his meal.

"Pay no mind to him, Eloisa." She drops my hand in favor of Leo's. "This is a wonderful thing." Her eyes are shiny with tears as she hugs me once more before leading us back to the family table.

Once seated, the waiter brings us *caffè* and *cornetti*. Leo stills my hands on my lap as I attempt to lay a napkin there. My fingers curl around him for just a moment.

"You look beautiful this morning," he says. I blush and smile at him. I expect a reaction from my family, but they don't say a word. I'm realizing that I have no idea how to act as an engaged woman. Anita and Dino never shied away from being in love publicly, but besides them, I've hardly gathered experience. I've only ever known Leo.

The conversation flows from one topic to the next. If my parents are dreading leaving our homeland, they aren't showing it. I shovel another bite of buttered *cornetti* into my mouth as my father looks at his watch.

"We'll want to be heading down to the docks soon," he says simply.

The lightheartedness of the morning suddenly grows dark. As if my mother finally realizes what's to become of us, she places her napkin on the table, scoops up baby Gino from his highchair, and leaves the table.

Lucia's eyebrows shoot up at our mother's sudden departure. "Wait for me, Mamma!" I watch as she slips her little hand into mother's and disappears around the corner.

"I'll meet you outside," Leo says, leaning over to kiss me on the cheek. He squeezes my hand and with a smile pushes back from the table.

I fold my napkin and place it on the table, fully intending to follow the others upstairs. My father reaches across the table and latches onto my wrist. I suck in a breath and look down. I don't know what I did wrong, but I'm sure I'm about to find out.

"I'm proud of you, Eloisa." I glance up, looking for the lie, but he's genuine. His eyes are softer than I've seen them in a long time. His hand wraps around my fingers and he gently squeezes. A man of few words, he leaves it be.

"*Grazie*, Papà." I smile at him and squeeze his hand back. When was the last time he and I had a moment like this? Before the war most likely. He blinks away the tears in his eyes and let's go.

Leo meets me outside just as he said. The sun has decided to light our way this afternoon, and I am grateful for it — nothing would have been worse than a stormy or even a dreary departure. Suddenly feeling the impending goodbyes, I try to take in every detail around me.

"How different is America?" I ask.

Leo wraps an arm around me and takes my large suitcase in his free hand. "It's different." Seeing the sudden fear on my face, he continues. "It's not a bad different at all, it's just —"

"Different?" I finish for him. He shrugs and nods.

"New York is a lot more crowded than anything you're used to. But there's a certain feeling about it that can feel like home at times. There's an awful lot of us out there you know."

I did know. Since the start of the decade, it was as if a family left Bari every week. None of them ever came back.

We sit on a bench a few feet from the hotel lobby. Looking down the hill toward the harbor, a chill runs down my back. I've been out on open water, but not far, and certainly not on a boat such as those big ocean liners that bob quietly next to the docks.

"How was the trip over?" I ask, trying to pry more information from him. He's never been one hold back a retelling of one of his adventures, but for some reason he's kept a tight lip on his most recent one.

"Boring."

"Certainly not," I scold.

He laughs with that heavy bellow that I've missed so much. "It wasn't as adventurous as the last crossing, I can say that." I loop my arm around his and nudge closer. The first trip to America had almost killed him, an unfortunate accident that could have turned deadly had the crew not known what to do. "The ships now are so much nicer. I'm telling you, the artwork aboard —" He loses his words. "You're gonna love it," he says in English and in a decidedly pretend American accent.

"Artwork?" No one had said anything about art.

Leo throws an arm out into space as if he were about to paint me a picture himself. "I can't speak for what's on the Andrea Doria, but I do know that Giulio Minoletti designed some of the interiors."

The name of the famous architect takes me by surprise, so much so that I backhand Leo in the chest. "You're kidding!"

"Not kidding," he says, trapping my belligerent hand in his. "We'll explore it all, together."

I lean in for a kiss and he reciprocates. Holding the back of my head gently, he brushes his lips against mine and then holds me tightly to him. I let my nerves subside. In his arms, there's no reason to worry about anything. Here I am safe.

CHAPTER TEN

Arden

July 18, 1956
MS Stockholm, Atlantic Ocean

Even a downer such as I can't stay below deck on a day like today. The sun shines brightly, and the water is clear and calm as we pick up the pace to New York. The upper decks have incurred life at last. Even with an easy first half of the voyage, many passengers are just now overcoming their seasickness and venturing out for the first time since leaving port. Kids play games while their parents stroll down the covered decks. It's summer, and with air conditioning still needing to be installed, on deck is the most comfortable place to be.

Many of my crewmates are out as well, despite whatever crazy schedule they must abide by. Crewmen have finally traded in their woolen jackets for short-sleeved button-ups and khakis. Groups of them walk by, nodding or saluting me in passing. Others mingle amongst the adventuring passengers, doing their best to make them feel welcome.

I cross a group of three on my way to the starboard side. Chief Officer Gustaf Källback is one of them. As he stalks past, all employee heads go down. The last thing anyone wants is the attention of our Chief Officer. A man of few words, Källback usually opens his mouth to reprimand. I try to look busy, but to my horror, he turns back to me after he's passed. Conversations between mates cease and men slink away from us. Despite the sudden clearance, I know every able-bodied seaman is listening closely nearby. I stand up straight and give the appropriate salute.

He dismisses me quickly and pulls a telegram from his pocket, well not a telegram, a note. "You've been excused from your evening duties," he says, handing it over. My brow furrows and my heart leaps to all sorts of conclusions as my eyes adjust to the petite lettering.

Mr. Lund,

I am extremely grateful for how you took care of my children the other day. They have not stopped speaking of you, and I believe they would like to see you again. I hope that you will accompany the children and I to dinner this evening. I know you are extremely busy, but Mr. Dawe assured me he would get this into your hands. If it pleases you, please dine with us tonight.

    Sincerely,

    Maja Larsen

I fold up the paper and tuck it into my back pocket. Källback has been watching me read the note and inevitably knows I'm about to find an excuse.

He holds up a hand before I can speak. "No getting out of it Lund. Captain's orders." My small good deed had reached the captain.

"Yes, sir."

He turns on his heel and leaves before I can even salute him. I huff to myself and trudge toward the starboard side lifeboats. I contemplate pitching the letter it into the ocean, but I know it won't solve my predicament. If anything, the young mother is trying to be nice, unaware of the discomfort it puts me in. Before this confrontation with Källback, I was perfectly fine with the captain not knowing that I exist; it's how I like things, an absence of attention.

Missing a round of duties doesn't sit right with me, but if Captain Nordenson knows, if he's approved it, I don't have a choice. I'll owe some sorry sap who takes up my round a drink or two. No one wants to take on an extra set of duties here, not with the slim number of deckhands we have this trip.

Even if I wanted to spend a meal in a crowded dining hall with a single mother and her children, I don't think I'd find it enjoyable. Work has always soothed my soul, while nights with strangers have always acted more like torture. I don't even know if I own anything appropriate for tonight. The fact that they're traveling in tourist class helps, but then again, I better just wear my uniform. No need to overthink the evening.

I get back to what relaxes me the most, working. Letting the minutes tick away, I focus on my mundane tasks — a pull of a lifeboat rope here, the push of a deck chair there. When was the last time I broke my daily pattern? Have I done anything out of my schedule in the last eight years? Looking out at sea, I laugh to myself. Since I boarded this ship on its maiden voyage, it's been nothing but following orders and suffering for the mistakes of my past.

Sighing, I have a seat on a foldable deck chair and watch as passengers come and go, happily conversing and laughing with each other. There are so many things I wish I could experience in this world, many things as simple as going on a stroll with a friend and laughing about frivolous things. I don't remember the last time I genuinely laughed.

A family stops at the rail near me, the father squats down beside his daughter and points into the water, explaining to her what he saw. I feel a twinge in my heart, so I avert my eyes. I wish I had moments like that with family to hold on to. I know my family is looking down at me from above and wishing I'd move on, to go and enjoy the company of a sweet family for dinner instead of worrying over my rounds. Instead of their lovely voices, I hear my own nagging monologue, telling me to keep my punishment going.

CHAPTER ELEVEN

Adeline

July 18, 1956
New York City, United State of America

The city seems so full in the mornings with everyone rushing everywhere all at once. My daughters and I add to the chaos as we hail a cab in a sea of strangers looking to do the same. Today we're heading from our hotel on Staten Island to Manhattan, where we'll shop and sightsee. I visited the borough by myself years ago but didn't have the urge to buy things then. New York really hasn't changed as much as I thought it would. It is always packed, and people always seem to be in a hurry.

After a lengthy journey, the girls are zapped of energy when the car comes to a stop at the corner of 6th Avenue and West 35th Street. I pay the driver and spill out onto the street with the crowd. The girls look up at the buildings in awe.

"Where are we?" Juliet asks.

Needing to beat the streetlight, I grab their hands and we hustle across along with a herd of other eager shoppers. We reach the world's flagship department store. With eleven floors for shopping, and a building the size of a city block, many people consider it the biggest store in the world, and they wouldn't be lying.

"Maman, where are we?" Juliet asks again, her attention taken by the garden in front of the store.

Knowing they're both intimidated, I hold them close to me. "We're going to go shopping in the big store."

They shuffle their feet forward, trying to keep up with the crowd. A twinge of guilt creeps in when I look at their nervous faces. They've only ever been to the local stores in France and the farmer's market in my hometown. I had wondered if I might do the shopping myself, but I knew Martin would never agree to watch the girls for a day, and frankly, I don't know if he would even know what to do with them for a few hours. A mother's job is never done; it can't ever be, otherwise the world would come undone.

As I lead them inside, their overwhelmed expressions are thankfully replaced by wonder. My own expectations are hard-pressed by the sheer amount of things stuffed into the lobby. Crowded? Sure. But nothing is put in its spot without a careful strategy. The store leads your sight in lines from left to right and top to bottom. There is not a single wasted display.

Johanna, Juliet, and I fit right in with the other women and children strolling through the aisles. The only men in the store wear suits and wander the floor looking for guests to help, or rather sell to. I let the girls each pick out a toy and a sweet treat. Each goes for a lollipop. Sticky, but it will keep their attention while I shop for Martin. I want to get him something nice, but every time I find an object he'd like, I either second-guess myself or find it to be too expensive. I would never buy myself something so nice. Especially not on a trip meant for buying gifts.

When we reach the back of the second floor, I realize we've been here two hours. Frustrated and pressed for time, I scoop my daughters into the cart. Going a bit quicker now, we run into the Rolex section of the store. Slowing to a browsing speed, my eye settles on a silver wristwatch. Stepping up to the display case, a young retailer hurries over. Obviously sensing prey, he places his hands behind his back and leans over to look at the case with me.

"Would you like me to get it out for you?"

Knowing he won't take no for an answer, I nod with a smile. "Yes, I'd love to take a look." Hopefully, this one will suffice because I don't want to spend the rest of my day here with this man telling me everything there is to know about every piece in the store. I drown out his speech as I watch him flip it over in his hand multiple times. Back in France, I could have it customized for him. If only I can hide it that long, or at least keep him from snooping until then. Thinking my plan out and realizing I'm ready to return home, I decide the watch is as good as any. "I'll take it," I say.

The man looks taken aback by the easy sale, but he walks us over to the register where a woman with a painted-on smile takes over. I know the look all too well. As the two converse about the purchase, I notice a bruise on the girl's cheek. My heart suddenly races.

I turn to my girls quickly, not wanting them to see anything amiss and comment on it. "This is a surprise for your father, okay." I hold a finger up to my lips to signify the secrecy.

They nod with their pure little smiles and giggle.

"All right ma'am, Susanna will be your cashier. I'm Daniel if you should need any more assistance."

The woman rings up my items, and I manage to not search her skin for any more signs of mistreatment. As a nurse and as a woman, it's hard for me not to notice the afflictions. They've become more and more common in the years following the war. I try to imagine the woman having a way out, but I come up empty. Instead, I shift my gaze and think of my own fortunate situation. Of course I wish things could be different in my home, but when I see alternatives like these, it makes me think twice about how truly fortunate I am.

"Do you want this gift wrapped?" she asks, rolling up her sleeves. I notice more bruises on her arms, these ones are a deep yellow.

"Yes, please," I stutter, trying not to wince, trying to think of something off-topic to say. When I can't find the right words quick enough, her hands go to cover her wrists. In two quick motions, she pulls her blouse sleeve back down. I hate that she's noticed me staring.

The woman bags my purchases and places them into my cart without saying a word. Knowing I can't recover from what I've already done, I take my things and thank her. She holds the bottom of her sleeves tight to her palms, only turning away after I've placed everything in my cart. As I wheel away, I can't help but wonder how it must be to come into work every day and giftwrap other women's suburban dreams in pretty paper and sparkly bows. I wouldn't be able to take it.

My mind is occupied on the way out of the store and the entire ride back to the apartment. Thankfully, the girls don't notice anything amiss, so they leave me be as we ride through Hoboken. My arms are tightly wound around my stomach, thinking about how fortunate I am to have a man who, despite his flaws, would never do something to hurt me.

Arriving back at our flat mid-afternoon, I expect it to be empty, but when I open the door, I find Martin at the kitchen table.

"You're home," he says with a grin. The girls push past me to their father who sits one girl on each thigh. "I was thinking you left me for good," he teases.

"Don't joke like that," I say, rounding the table and kissing him on the cheek.

"I hope you got me something good," he says, squeezing both girls, looking for answers.

"We did!" Juliet spills. Johanna scowls at her. "But we can't tell you what it is until Maman says we can."

Martin raises his eyebrow. "Is that so?"

I reach into my bag and retrieve his box. "No snooping."

He holds his hands up in defense. I know he thinks he's innocent of it, but he's notorious for finding every Christmas and birthday present I attempt to give him.

"Hey girls, why don't you go play, I'm going to talk to your maman for a second."

"What's wrong?" I ask as the girls run off to their room.

"Nothing, my love." He moves closer to me and reaches for my hands. "I know you just got home and might be tired after a long day of shopping, but there is a reason I'm home so early."

"And what's that?" I ask, rising to my toes to give him a kiss.

"I've planned an evening for us," he says as he pulls me in tighter, responding to my kiss.

I pull back to look at him. "I'm not tired but the girls —"

"They're staying here."

"What?" I ask, pushing back further.

Martin chuckles and pulls his hands up in defense, "I've got it all planned. There's a nanny on staff and we could —"

"Honey, slow down," I say, laying an unsure hand on his chest.

"You don't want to go?" Martin's face slides with disappointment, the last thing I want to see from him, ever.

Though, my first reaction is worry over the girls being alone with a stranger, I know that I desperately need a night out with him. "Yes, of course I want to go."

I pause a moment, deciding if I want to know the plans, but then decide I don't. I don't want to spoil the surprise."

A smile spreads across his face. "I just wanted one evening alone with you before we leave."

"Me too," I say as he plants a kiss on my forehead.

With one quick squeeze, he lets me go. A million different things run through my head as I pad through the living room to our bedroom, including ideas of what I should wear out. Martin has always been full of surprises, I need to learn not to doubt him.

CHAPTER TWELVE

Eloisa

July 18, 1956
SS Andrea Doria, Mediterranean Sea

We are engulfed in a world of splendor as we cross the threshold of the gangway to the ship. To my trained eye, the work of famous Italian architects is noticeable immediately. Everything from the mosaic on the wall to the furniture is impeccably sleek and modern.

Leo nudges me. "What did I tell you?"

"Yes, it's marvelous," I say, my eyes diverting to the ceiling so full of color it could be the sky itself.

We're assigned a block of three rooms on C-deck and are given two sets of keys for each cabin. Now that our hands are full with keys, brochures, and daily itineraries, we're pushed along to allow the next group to be welcomed. Father seems clueless as to how to navigate the ship, so we look to Leo who is already running his fingers across the number on his key.

"Well C-deck," he says before looking at the number again. "My guess would be the starboard side." I knew port and starboard were terms for the sides of a ship, but I could never keep the two straight.

My parents haven't spoken since we boarded, and even now they let Leo lead us without so much as a nod. It's the look of many who are boarding with us, old Italians leaving their home for the prospect of America. It's quite sad actually; it brings down the grandeur of the ship. If it weren't for Leo beaming with every possibility, I might just cry myself.

When we reach our hallway and subsequent cabins, we take a collective breath and enter. Lucia immediately blows past me and launches herself onto the bed closest to the hull.

"Is this mine?" She delights as she bounces up and down. I take my suitcase and place it on the other bed.

"Whatever you want," I say with a smile. Her face lights up as she falls back and sprawls across the now rumpled bedding. Tonight will be the first time she'll have her own bed to sleep in. In the past, she's either climbed in with me or slept in a heap of cushions and blankets on the floor.

Returning to the hallway to collect the rest of the luggage, Leo meets me at the door and passes them off to me. "What do you think, little Lucia?" he asks, leaning against the door frame. She stands and starts to bounce all over the bed once again.

"Don't encourage her," I say as I stifle a laugh.

I turn to the small dresser at the far side of the room and start neatly tucking my clothes in. Lucia joins me a minute later and tosses hers in, completely undoing the precise packing mother had done this morning.

As I take on the rest of the organization, Lucia flounces to our parent's neighboring room, dragging Leo with her. The doors out in the hallway are left gaping open as more and more people arrive. A collage of languages spills out of them. Across from me an older couple speaks Italian, while a young woman and her mother pass speaking in crystal clear English. From my family's block of rooms comes a combination of both.

I smile to myself as I shove my largest suitcase underneath the bed. Laying back on the soft comforter, I stare up at the ceiling. With the chores done, I grab my sketchbook and outline the room quickly. I want to remember every moment of this journey.

My quick sketch quickly turns from an outline into a detailed drawing of the cabin, everything from the pattern of the carpet to the swirls in the mahogany dresser. I become so invested in the spontaneous inspiration that I don't notice Leo until he's standing right in front of me, blocking my view of the furthest wall.

"Don't you think we could find something more interesting for you to draw?" he asks, extending a hand to me.

I pull my book closer to me and place the pencil in the crease. I choose to challenge him. "What did you have in mind?" I raise my eyebrows, pretending to doubt that anything could be more fascinating than this very room.

He reaches for my hand and pulls me up without an answer. I grab the room keys and push them deep into a pocket, preventing any escape. We pause at my parent's room briefly. Inside they sit on their respective beds, and mother clutches Gino to her as if they're too scared to move. Lucia is on the floor flipping through the ship's catalog.

"We're going exploring," I say in passing, hoping for some kind of response. Getting none but concerned looks, I drop the extra key on a cushioned chair and bolt back to the hallway before Lucia can tag along.

"I don't understand how they can be so rigid, so un-invested," I mention some time after emerging on the top deck. We pulled out to open water almost two hours ago and my parents still haven't left their room. "That's the last time we might ever see Italy, and they couldn't even come up on deck to wave goodbye."

"Everyone handles fear differently," Leo says, squeezing my hand and brushing my knuckles against his lips. "They'll come to terms with it in time, or maybe they won't." He shrugs.

"They'll never get that moment back." I look back out to sea, and for a moment, I think I see a speck of home, but it's a trick of the eyes.

"Then they'll have to live with it." He emphasizes the 'they'll'. I know I can't be the one with the hurting heart for their mistakes, but after everything our family has been through, it would have been nice to toss it all behind us together.

"Would you like to get some dinner, *amore mio*?"

As if my stomach is urging me to answer, it grumbles. I haven't eaten since breakfast. Shaking my head free of remorse, I slip my arm into Leo's as we follow the crowd to the tourist class dining room.

The room is buzzing with conversations, again a mixture of languages. A waiter seats us with a family of four. They welcome us with warm smiles, the straw-blond hair of the daughter and mother gives them away before they even open their mouths. They're American.

"Hiya sugar," the mother says, patting me on my shoulder. It's an accent I've only heard in the movies. As our waiter pours water into our crystal glasses, I get caught staring at this perfectly modern family in front of me. "You speak English hun?" The mother is again speaking, unfolding her napkin and placing it in her lap.

"She does," Leo says with a laugh. "A little star-struck by her first trip away from home." A slap on the back brings words back to my mouth.

"Aw, well that would leave one tongue-tied, wouldn't it?" The mother takes a sip, her perfect red lips leaving smudges on the glass.

"Well darling, I'm awfully glad you've joined our table," she reaches next to her with her painted nails and latches on to her husband's wrist. "My husband isn't the most talkative over dinner." Taking another sip, the conversation runs dry until I make the move of folding my hands in plain view of the table.

"Your ring is beautiful." The daughter, a spitting image of her mother, gasps and waves her hand at me. I let her take my hand and she stares hard at it.

"Let it be a lesson to you Joanie, never settle for less." The mother flashes her golden band and her husband rolls his eyes with an affectionate smile.

We become quite acquainted with the Baker family throughout the meal. From Savannah, Georgia, they'd been traveling to see Rome. The husband, Jack, had been stationed there toward the end of the war. Joanie and Jonah, twins, are nearing high school and excel in academics. The mother, Marjorie, is a beacon of light, a woman I could only aspire to be.

Upon their leave, Leo asks the waiter to have the kitchen send three meals to my parent's cabin. I'm alight with love for him, always thinking of others, he is the definition of selfless. I can't believe I'm lucky enough to have him looking out for me for the rest of my life.

There's some dancing in the tourist class ballroom, but I never learned how to. Growing up in a small village, I never got the chance. Knowing this, Leo pulls me past the open doors to the lido deck where some other couples have spilled out. It's a lot less crowded here and the setting is more intimate. I grab my book from my bag and sit in the nearest chair. Leo sits beside me without a word. I draw what I see: dazzling lights, couples huddling close together as they sway to imaginary music much slower than what's being played in the ballroom, and the moonlight reflecting perfectly off the outdoor swimming pool's cerulean water below.

Feeling overwhelmed by the romance of it, I let my pencil still and turn slowly to the man beside me. He's staring at me, his eyes glowing brighter than the pool below. We stare at each other for a moment. We are here, together, in this magical place on our way to our new life. He flashes a smile and leans into me. Resting a warm hand on my cheek, he kisses me. He's still smiling as he pulls away, and his eyes are glowing with hunger. I want to suggest something, something that I shouldn't. I open my mouth to speak, but I'm saved from compromising myself due to the music changing. The hunger in his expression dissipates in exchange for recognition. I perk up my ears but don't why he'd know the song.

"It's 'Pledging My Love'," he says, expecting me to suddenly understand. "Johnny Ace?" He pauses again. "I saw him once in person, in New York." I slump a little bit, there's still so much I don't know about his life there. He ignores my sudden sullenness and hops to his feet. "It's a great song!" He pulls me up and twirls me away from him and then back to him again. I feel the heat rising, my embarrassment rising with it. I try to step away from him, but he keeps a lock on my hand. "It's an easy song to dance to, c'mon, I'll show you. Eloisa, it's okay to be comfortable with me."

I don't trust my skill, but I do trust him. He's right, I shouldn't be afraid to bare all my insecurities to him. Taking a deep breath, I nod and step back within an inch of him. He holds me close as we sway back and forth. The only person's opinion that I care about is Leo's, and he doesn't care about my lack of dance instruction at all. I loosen up after I realize he's not looking at my feet or my form like boys do in magazines, instead, he's holding my gaze.

The band switches to an attempt at "Heartbreak Hotel", a song I do recognize. With the lead singer doing his best impression of Elvis, people pick up the pace. This time I approach the dance with confidence, something that surprises Leo. We break apart, mimicking the movements of those around us. More people have danced their way out on the deck, escaping the heat from inside. Everyone is carefree, smiling, and happy. This has to be the happiest night of my life, or certainly the prettiest.

When the final song of the night finishes, there's collective applause from the dancers. The band takes their bows and start to pack up. It's hard not to dance back to my room, the music still vibrating through every fiber of my being. I lay my head on Leo's shoulder, and he hugs me close as we walk stride for stride.

"When we get to New York, I'll take you dancing every night," he whispers. Scenes of glorious nights out under the lights of New York City flash before my eyes.

"We've come a long way since the cupboard." The statement causes us both to stop. Tension spreads. "I'm sorry I shouldn't have brought it up."

I try to shrug it off, but the fact of the matter is I've fought every day to forget the night in the cupboard. "You're right we have."

Despite the terror we went through on December 2, 1943, it's where our story began. I suppose I should make an effort to appreciate that fact.

"Despite it all, Eloisa, I'm glad that horrid night went the way it did." My stomach twists. How could I ever betray my community by claiming that night as a positive in my life? "I wouldn't change it."

I swallow hard. "I'm glad you were there." It's the only truth I can admit to.

CHAPTER THIRTEEN

Arden

July 18, 1956
MSS Stockholm, Atlantic Ocean

"Relax a little bit Lund," Curt Dawe says from behind his glass. On his command, I let my shoulders slump and lean toward the table.

Dinner with the passengers has put me on edge. When the Larsen family appears in the doorway of the tourist class dining room, the tension feeds into me at full force. Small talk is something one has to practice being good at, and I've only ever practiced avoiding it. A passenger dining room is another thing I have relentlessly tried to stray away from.

Dawe, ever the natural life of the party, stands and greets the three travelers as they make their way over. He pulls out a chair for Ms. Larsen, who offers a confident smile as she sits. The kids climb into the chairs; they have to sit on their knees in order to see over the dining table. Little Kirsten and Thomas are shy at first, hardly glancing my way. When the mother opens her mouth, the sweetest sound tumbles from it. She speaks in a beautiful combination of our native tongue and English, which takes me back home. She can't be more than twenty, and yet, she radiates motherhood. She reaches across the table and takes my hand in hers, instantly calming me.

As the night continues, the roles of who's shy and who's confident appear to switch. After the appetizer, Ms. Larsen becomes quiet, shy even, while the children now do most of the talking, volleying between telling our little party random facts and changing the topic every other minute. I sit back and let the food and drink run freely. To peer into the life of a family for an evening is altogether soothing — and all too much to handle. I feel myself swallowing back a wave of emotion before hiding behind my drink. The burn of the alcohol instantly stops the tears from forming.

I'm able to make it through the rest of the courses without incident. As the waiter starts to clear the dessert, the kids escape their seats and run around the table to my chair. They both wrap their arms around me in a hug, and then they do the same to Curt. The mother smiles before gathering her kids and leaving us with one more, "Thank you."

I bid my farewell to Curt and take my leave, escaping back outside and toward familiarity. The cool, salty air hits me, but the leftover tension from the dinner resides. Without much contemplation, I fall right back into my rounds. Of course, someone covered for me while I was at dinner, but it won't hurt to double-check everything. For my own sanity, and to keep with my routine, I walk my route and keep an eye out for missed details. To my annoyance, everything is done perfectly. I sigh, reminding myself that I'm one of a million sailors throughout the world that knows how to do what I do. Sometimes, I forget how much of a surplus men are out here at sea.

Many nations saw an entire generation killed during the war. But many of the survivors that returned made their way to the open ocean when they saw how different life was back home. Sailing gives me a sense of discipline, routine, and above all, it's something to be proud of. But more recently, I've noticed men my age have started to disappear, have chosen to return to their homelands. Everybody's sorrow has an expiration date, some hold on to it until death, but nonetheless it still ends. It seems that a lot of those around me have decided to let go of their sadness in exchange for a chance at happiness.

What excuse do I have that they don't? Why do I hold on? Regret? I'm sure they all have it, but I view my own as something that I'll never get past. I can't bring myself to go back home because of it, especially when it still causes me to wither away out here day after day.

Tonight, I sat with a mother traveling alone with her two children. If she can pack up everything and move to a new country, surely I can find my way back to where it all started. I've forced myself to think about the possibility of returning before, but it always ends the same way, with Nora's beautiful face and soft smile screaming into my head. I hang my head low between my outstretched arms to try and move past her, but she's the block in my mind that causes me to deteriorate from the outside in.

When I realize my nails are digging into my palms, I release the tension and all thoughts of returning to Sweden. It's not a question of whether I deserve this or not, as the answer is quite clear to me: I believe that my punishment has not yet been served, and perhaps it never will.

CHAPTER FOURTEEN

Adeline

July 18, 1956
New York City, United States of America

"I just worry about the girls."

"Adeline," Martin says, caressing my fingers in his. "They're fine. I gave Judith and the hotel the name and number of the restaurant before we left. If anything were to happen, we're right down the street."

I've never spent more than an hour away from them, and now as the evening gives way to night in the big city, my motherly nerves rear their ugly head. I hate to hint to Martin that I want to cut the evening short, considering I've had such a marvelous time with him, but I miss my girls.

Martin's big surprise night out was truly what I needed. It was a chance for me to get out of my day dresses and wear something glamorous. Even though I've fretted about the girls throughout the evening, I can't ignore how being on Martin's arm, and all dressed up, has made me feel.

We had front-row tickets to My Fair Lady at the Mark Hellinger Theatre, which was elegant and captivating. Even in my best dress I still felt like a rhinestone amongst an audience of diamonds. But no matter, it was a night to celebrate two small-town lovers in a big city. We've always been small-town kids at heart. The war forced us to be well-traveled, and I wouldn't change it for anything, but at the end of the day, we'd still hope for a chance at a quiet life. At least I hope he still wants that. I know I do.

For dinner, he reserved a window seat table at a restaurant a block away from where my girls are. The food was eaten long ago, but for whatever reason, Martin drags his feet in leaving. Being so close to the hotel causes me to want to be with them again, so I try to push him along again. "Darling," I begin. "I have truly enjoyed our evening, but don't you think we should be getting back?"

"You are gorgeous." His comment takes me off guard. He was always a man of subtle romance, of gestures and looks, but never of comments. "It's been so long since we've had any time to ourselves." I want to rebut, but of course I cannot. "I hope, of course, that more nights like these are in our future," he finishes.

I almost fall for it. The sweetness of today, his attention to my happiness, the way he tended to the girls earlier. I swallow the last drop of champagne in my glass and the golden aura around him fades to the wayside. "What's all this about, Martin?" I set my glass down in order to study him properly. Months of nothing but sulking in the corner and then today a complete change of heart.

"You've caught me," he says it with a chuckle, but I don't get the joke. "Adeline, I've been waiting for the right time to tell you this …" My heart stops beating. Anything could come next. "You know I've been to several meetings during our time in the city."

"Yes." It's all I can muster, my hands tensing, my lungs barely expanding to let in air.

"They're looking to invest in a new branch in Barcelona." He pauses, waiting for an answer, but I can't bring myself to speak. What is he implying? "They want me to lead the whole thing. Be the first boots on the ground, so to speak." There's that stupid chuckle again.

I push back from the table and grip the edge to steady myself, feeling the need to bolt. "You're saying that you're going to leave us here?"

"No, darling —"

"You'll leave us at home in France then?"

"No," he says, puzzled. "It's my wish that you all would come with me."

Realizing that I've drawn attention to our intimate scene, I smooth my dress and politely sit back down. Spain. Another move. Another country. Another language. Another change.

"They're fairing pretty well right now," Martin continues. "We want in before everyone else finds their way there."

I turn to meet his gaze. "Do you understand what you are asking of me?"

I watch his face flatten. "I'm asking you to support me in this endeavor."

"Please don't ask me to do this Martin."

"Why?"

My heart lurches. I could bare all my fears to him here in this restaurant, but I shouldn't have to. France is bad enough, being so far from home, speaking a language my four-year-old daughters know better than me, reliving the war every day, left to do nothing but care for the girls. He should know these are my demons. He should know. Why doesn't he know? When I can't bring myself to answer, his features turn from unreadable to undoubtedly sad. I can't seem to swallow my pride to tell him. I desperately want to tell him, but I want him to understand the unspoken even more.

He sighs. "Perhaps we can revisit the notion when we get home in a few weeks." The way he says home drives one final spear through my heart before he moves behind my chair and tugs it away from the table. He takes my arm and escorts me out into the city night.

I have to fight tears the whole walk back. If Martin notices my sniffles, he doesn't acknowledge them, just holds me against him tightly. I've let him down, I know that, but hasn't he done the same to me? I try to calm myself. He wouldn't have asked this of me if he didn't truly believe we could thrive there. Perhaps it's not final, perhaps there is a way to talk him out of it.

As we enter the hotel lobby, I have a revelation. I'm not scared of starting over, I've done it time and time again. I realize that I'm scared of being stuck in a country I know nothing about. Scared of unhappiness. Scared that Martin won't have the time to nurture our family with me. I glance over at my husband as the elevator operator punches our number. The happiness I've felt today outweighs any of the tough stretches we've ever had together. I married him for a reason, and those vows I made are permanent. I just hope he remembers his promises, too.

I grab his hand to stop him when we exit onto our floor. Staring up at him, I study his face, neither of us speaks. He's too stubborn to ask me what's going on, and I'm too obedient to push the matter any further. When I can't hold his attention any longer, I step out of his way. He drops my hand and pushes past me, leaving me alone in the hallway. There was a time when I thought I could be happy with him anywhere, but I'm realizing that that reality is becoming harder and harder to achieve.

CHAPTER FIFTEEN

Eloisa

July 19, 1956
SS Andrea Doria, Mediterranean Sea

A new day dawns, and the Andrea Doria is alive with people from all over the world. The sun has just begun to peak over the waves, and my family has already been up for an hour. It's as if we haven't quite shaken the notion that we will be taken care of during this voyage. There are no morning chores for us to do and no errands to run. Of course, I would not have minded sleeping in for once, but Lucia and my parents had other plans. Hopefully, my parents will indulge in the luxury on this voyage because I'd like to try it at least once while I'm out here.

Leo doesn't answer when I gently knock on his door. I stifle a laugh and smile to myself as I walk away, he's always been a heavy sleeper. When I enter the dining room, my American friends are nowhere to be seen.

Breakfast is an assortment of eggs, oatmeal, biscuits, fruit, and beverages. I can't believe how fresh it all tastes. It surprises Mamma as well, it's all over her face in the widening of her eyes. Come to think of it, I don't think my mother has ever had this many meals in a row that she didn't have a hand in making. Encouraged by her reaction, I feel a weight lift off my shoulders. I'm not so naive as to believe that I am the sole reason for our move, but it has been a burden to think that my engagement was the final straw for my family to uproot everything and move away.

The mood quickly stiffens when Gino starts to wail and proceeds to spit up.

"Poor dear doesn't like the movement of the ocean," Papà says as he pats his lips with his napkin.

"He never was soothed by rocking," Mamma says, holding him tightly to her chest.

"Perhaps we could all go up to the deck after breakfast and get some fresh air," I suggest.

My parents both give me pointed looks as if I'd asked them if they all would jump right into the ocean with me. I hear Leo's remarks from the day buzzing in one ear and out the other, 'Everyone handles fear differently'.

"Lucia and I will go then." I push back my chair and grab my sister's hand. "I'll check back in with you later." Like good daughters do, we both kiss our parents goodbye and head for the door at a womanly pace.

"Why are they so square?" Lucia says, letting the American phrase roll off her tongue a little too easily.

"Square?" I stare down at my little sister, wondering where she could have heard it. "Have you been reading my magazines?"

"I can't read," she shrugs. "I heard a blonde girl use it yesterday."

I shake my head at my little sister. She is perfectly capable, the smartest seven-year-old I've ever met. I roll my eyes and push her along.

The Mediterranean sun beats down on Lucia and I as we recline on the lido deck. From our position on the poolside chairs, we watch as women stroll by in bikinis and sunglasses. The pool is chock-full of mid-morning swimmers, some tossing a beach ball. We don't have a care in the world. But while I'm perfectly content locking my fingers behind my head and relaxing, my sister watches our shipmates with wild eyes. It's like she can't gather enough information quickly enough.

"There you ladies are!" I go to shield my eyes from the sun, but Leo has already cast his shadow, saving me the effort. I pull my bare feet in and tuck my dress around me. I pat the edge of my deck chair and he has a seat.

He's wearing solid blue shorts and an unbuttoned striped shirt that rests over a white undershirt. He runs his fingers through his hair and sets his drink aside.

Leaning forward he steals a kiss and grins. "I'm sorry I missed breakfast this morning."

"That's all right," I say, returning his smile. "Lucia and I made our escape quite quickly."

"That bad?" His smile falters slightly.

"Mamma and Papà are squares," Lucia says, desperately wanting in on our conversation. I roll my eyes.

"Someone's been reading her sister's magazines," Leo says, pinching her cheek. Lucia scowls, while I try my best to hide my smile. Leaving the topic behind, Leo leans back. "Would you girls want some shaved ice?"

Lucia shoots up out of her deck chair. *Granita* is what we call it at home, and we've never had the opportunity or the means to try it.

"I'd hate to give up this perfectly good spot in the sun," I fuss.

Leo winks. "I'll bring you one. Lemon still your favorite flavor?" My heart skips. Yes, lemon has been my favorite anything since I was a kid. I nod and he steals another kiss.

I fall back against my chair and stretch out. There's an amalgamation of soothing sounds humming in my ear. Laughter comes from the pool, the engines hum far below me, and there's soft music coming from inside. I pull out my sketchbook and start to draw, the white noise sucking me under.

"Well, hey there, Miss Eloisa!"

The sounds breaks my spell, and I look up to find Mrs. Baker and some other women strolling past me.

They don't stop to talk but they smile and wave, filling me with warmth. I'm quick to return the favor. I've decided this ship isn't so different from a small town. Everyone is polite to each other, at least here in tourist class, and by the end of the voyage, we will all know each other by name. But we can also all go about our day and experience the journey how we choose to. I take heart in the fact that, while change is brewing, perhaps this ship can act as a buffer to soften the blow.

When Leo returns with my sister, bringing samples of the sweet snack, I push my drawing away. The three of us sit together and indulge. It's safe to say that we never spent our money on treats like this at home, so to have such an overwhelming sweetness hit my tongue causes my teeth to hurt. The ache doesn't matter because the taste is so wonderful, and the people I'm sharing it with are equally appreciative of its power.

To douse our brain freezes the three of us leap into the warmed pool. As I come up from the initial plunge, I watch as Leo lifts Lucia onto his shoulders, sinks low into the water, and then lurches upward, tossing her high into the air. She comes out of the water laughing, begging him to do it again. It's not long before the other kids see it, soon Leo has a line of younger kids waiting their turn to fly through the water.

I swim to the edge and pull myself out of the water, watching the kids surrounding him. A pool attendant brings me a drink as I watch Leo's performance from my perch. When he looks over, I raise my glass to him and smile. He smiles back before quickly returning his attention to the children. I can't wait to have children of our own.

CHAPTER SIXTEEN

Arden

July 19, 1956
MS Stockholm, Atlantic Ocean

I wouldn't say I had the easiest go of things in the war, but I definitely didn't see the worst of humanity, like some of my crewmates. Many of my worst days came in the beginning, when I lost the only things I ever loved. When I was shipped out after that day, I didn't really care what happened to me. My missions are a blur, overshadowed by the biggest loss I've ever endured.

While we do have a few veterans who saw fierce fighting on land and sea alike, there are many that lucked out of experiencing the worst of the war. Half the men on this ship, if I could call them men, know nothing of war. They pretend that they do, and that makes it worse. It would have been one thing if they had kept to themselves about it, but it's another thing entirely to describe the experience as a damn vacation.

I sit back from the desk; I'm hunched over and rub my eyes. Lunch today had come to blows. Young against old, veteran against veteran. The two in the guilty party will surely be relieved of duty when we reach port, I'm surprised they've not been hauled away to the brig already. Despite what the outburst today may have insinuated, war is not an uncommon topic amongst us. We use it to bond, to understand one another. While Sweden remained a neutral power throughout the war, many of the Swedish men on this ship volunteered to go to Norway or Finland in the beginning. Others made the same mistake as I; they fled too early and ended up running headlong into a war in a foreign land.

At our meal, a young steward had grown too loud and confident while recalling his female conquests during his brief time enlisted near the end of the war. His one — of many — mistakes was being loud enough for the burly Norwegian Askel Nilsen to over-hear him. Nilsen is known for two things: the shadow he casts behind him, and that he was the only one of his brothers to survive the battles of Narvik.

I can't say I blame the man for his sudden burst of violence, I wasn't sure how much longer I could stand the audacity of the boy's adventures. The whole thing was over in seconds. Nilsen scraped his chair across the floor like a bolt of lightning and the kid's face was bashed in before anyone could swallow their bite of meatball. When fist hit bone, there was not a sound to be heard, besides the wailing of the young soldier. His nose gushed blood as he rolled around on the floor in pain. An officer rushed in and had Askel and the steward detained. As they were escorted out, the rest of the men looked back down at their food and ate their meals in silence — too many long-forgotten and long-unwanted memories had returned to the dining hall. The incident brought back my own painful memories, along with the reminder of one task I struggle to complete.

I've been sitting at this god-forsaken desk for hours and have yet to finish my letter. After hours of composing an apology to home, I have nothing to show for it. Writing to Nora's parents has been a long time coming. It'll most likely end up in the trash bin, like so many others, but sometimes carrying words of my native tongue in my pocket, no matter their content, makes me feel lighter.

My regrets and apologies are authentic, but it's impossible to imagine a reaction. No, it hurts to imagine one. How does one ask forgiveness after what I've done? My stomach starts to turn at the thought of my mistakes. I took her from her home and right into the thick of it, and then I left her again. The final kiss we shared still buzzes on my lips, and the thought of Klara's small hand in mine sends electricity through my fingers. The last time I saw them was September 7, 1940. Of course, no one could have known the Nazis would choose that night to start their Blitzkrieg over

London. I thought it would have been safer there, many of us did. It was until it wasn't.

I offer my silent apologies to the ceiling and tuck the letter deep into my trouser pocket. With a few words on paper, and no desire to throw it away, perhaps this one will finally escape my pocket once we reach port.

CHAPTER SEVENTEEN

Adeline

July 19, 1956
New York City, United States of America

Another day with the girls brings me back down to earth. Last night I was beside myself with worry, fretting about the future of my family, but my girls have a way of reminding me that my one true responsibility and purpose is to keep them happy and healthy. So that's what I focused on today. We baked cookies, we watched the television, we played with dolls, and we cooked their father's favorite dinner.

Their father never showed up.

He'd mentioned that he would be working into the evening, but I still expected him to be home by seven. The girls and I watched the pork get cold, and still we waited until our stomachs growled and the girls' eyes started to droop with sleep. Johanna ate in silence, but Juliet, ever the perceptive one, asked me where her father was three times. I didn't have a true answer for her. I knew he would be out working late, I knew it, but I suspected he'd make it a priority to eat dinner with us. I know he's frustrated with me, but that should never come between him and the girls. The worry from yesterday returned, and it's all I could think about for the rest of the meal.

After dinner, I get them washed, throw the leftovers into the fridge, and pin my hair up in rollers. Alone, I pour a glass of wine and peer out the window at the glistening city.

When I was fourteen, I stumbled across a picture of New York City on New Year's Eve, it was all glitz and glamour. I thought nothing would ever compare to that photo until I witnessed V-J Day in Times Square. I kissed multiple sailors that day, had a little too much to drink that night, and the next morning I hopped a train home. One month later, I was heading straight back to France with my future husband.

Sometimes I wonder what life would have been like if I had gone home with one of those sailors in Time Square instead. What if I had married Billy Collins down the road and settled on his family farm? Would I feel as trapped as I do right now? Would my skills still be ignored? I ran away with Martin because

I thought the thing I was most afraid of wouldn't be a problem with him. It turns out being a wife can be just as miserable with him as it would have been with any of the others. I clutch my wine glass tighter and try to imagine a situation where I would have been happy as a housewife. When nothing comes to mind, I remember why I was never meant to be officially tied down to anyone.

Suddenly frustrated by the glowing lights of the freedom below, I turn to the couch. The end of a new Lone Ranger episode is playing on the television, the volume barely at a buzz. Clayton Moore looks back at me, the masked man himself. I remember reading a headline in the paper when he'd enlisted in the Army. He and a few other filmmakers and actors were tasked with creating propaganda and training films for the boys. I think I saw one about radar once. How lucky that he could go back to doing what he loved after his experience in the army.

I sigh, and I am about to head to bed when the front door fans open. In comes six men, led by my husband. I grab my robe and wrap it tightly around my nightgown. I cross my arms across my chest and wait for an explanation.

When Martin stumbles forward my first guess is that he's drunk, and his friends have returned him to me. As he approaches the light, I realize that I am mistaken; he's just overwhelmingly happy. I tense up, unsure of the occasion. Angry that he can be so happy when I've been so miserable the past few hours waiting for him.

"Sorry, mademoiselle," a balding man says, his head dipping low. The rest of the men follow suit, averting their eyes from my robe-clad body. My heart softens, only slightly, when I realize the men are familiar to me, Martin's war buddies and business partners.

"Martin —"

"Just having a night out with the lads," he grumbles tersely.

I put my hands on my hips, trying to pass a hint that, as much as I love his coworkers and everything they yearn to accomplish, I'd rather not have them here at this hour. As I move into the kitchen, I recross my arms and lean against the countertop. "The girls are sleeping," I say, glancing at their cracked door.

"Ah yes." He turns to his friends, and they all let out deep laughter in response. Clearly, I'm not involved in their inside joke.

Embarrassed, and a tad hurt, I bite my lip and look down at my bare feet. There's nowhere for this conversation to go until Martin escorts them out. Regaining my composure, I elect to look up and stare my husband straight in the eye. I catch him nod slightly and then he's busy corralling his friends out the door. Once the door clicks into place, I step away from the counter, ready to fight for myself. "And what's the meaning of all this?" I ask, trying to keep a level head until I get an explanation.

Martin pulls the handle on the fridge, the room suddenly igniting with the glowing light from within. "Just a bit of fun that's all. Majority of them are going back to France tomorrow." He closes the door, the cold airflow coming to an abrupt end. "They're alone. You must understand how hard it still is to go back after what we went through over there."

I suck back my annoyance, knowing very well the trauma it causes us each time we disembark. I also know that Martin is beyond this stage. The partying and drinking dominated his life at the beginning of our marriage. I couldn't blame him, he had been cheated out of the prime of his life by the war. I was patient with him, and soon enough the late nights and wine fell away and were replaced with bedtime stories and family dinners. I guess old habits die hard.

"I wish you would have told me is all," I say, my hands folded in front of me, clinging to my restraint for dear life.

He leans forward and pecks me on the cheek before moving to the kitchen table to devour the cold leftovers I saved for him. I watch from the corner, holding out hope that he'll have more to say. When he refuses to look my way, I leave him there and head for bed.

I tuck myself in a little tighter than usual to deter the cold. I know he's frustrated, but I just don't know how we've gotten to this point. We both fought so hard for each other in the beginning. It wasn't an act, not on his part, and certainly not on mine. I just hope it wasn't a big scheme to coax me into an impossible paradise just to leave me alone to watch it all dissolve before my very eyes.

CHAPTER EIGHTEEN

Eloisa

July 20, 1956
SS Andrea Doria, Mediterranean Sea

This ship is a floating art gallery, just like Leo said. Up until today, I'd discovered some of the classic pieces in and around the tourist class areas. Now I'm checking off each painting and sculpture as I go on Leo's guided expedition through the ship. He woke me up bright and early. Starting at the lowest level available to passengers, we snaked our way through each deck. Somehow Leo was able to scout out the ship in our few days aboard. He keeps me moving, but never getting us lost once. My legs are exhausted, I don't think I've ever walked this much in my life.

Though I wasn't the one leading the tour, I did feel like the tour guide. The ship is adorned with many pieces by renowned Italian artists, and I feel honored to share my knowledge of them with Leo. Despite my ramblings of extra information for each piece, he insists that he'll take me to all the art galleries in New York. He tells me that I'll be mesmerized by the sheer number and size of them.

Most of the art on board are paintings hung on the wall, or murals that make up the wall itself. But none of them compare to our findings in the Winter Garden Lounge. I found the gem of the ship, the pieces that have the power to render me silent and staring for hours. It's a Guido Gambone, that much is clear. The 1,000-pound panels with ceramic sculptures span the walls from floor to ceiling. I've never seen anything like it, not in pictures and certainly not in person. Despite the well-dressed couples sipping on their martinis that pay no mind to it, I stand and study. The backgrounds are made of purple and red tiles, and the bold carvings of primitive art stand out on top. Stunning and provoking.

I don't know exactly how long I spent gaping, but eventually, Leo escorts me from the room. I'm not sure what causes him to do so, though perhaps it was the rude stares I was starting to gather, or perhaps it was the waiter with his hands on his hips. I won't ever know, the only thing I take with me from that gorgeous room of riches is the beauty of the walls.

"Wow," I say, looking out to sea. Looking back toward the stern, I can still see a bit of our last port, Gibraltar. Leo embraces me from behind, and I lay my head back against his chest. "Wow," I repeat, this time huffing out a laugh.

"Are you talking about our day viewing art or the view?" He asks, a chuckle reverberating against me.

"The art." I cock my head to the side, "Though I suppose the view is God's version of it, so both."

"Now that might be the first thing that you've said today that I truly understand," he says, leaning his head on mine.

I bite my lip. "I'm sorry," I say, turning to him. "I hope you weren't bored or annoyed."

He holds me tighter; I can hear the smile in his voice. "I wanted you to see everything. We've only got a few more days out here, I thought you might as well enjoy it." He leans in and whispers, "And I missed hearing you talk about art."

I playfully push him away. "I don't think you're telling the truth," I laugh. When we were younger, he would roll his eyes and shove fingers in his ears every time I spoke about any form of it.

"Okay, so I might have tuned you out once, but that's a record for me."

I cross my arms. "Was it the Giulio Minoletti beams in the entryway or —"

"It was a portrait in the dining room. A pretty girl caught my eye," he winks. He swoops me to the side and dips me low. Realizing how dramatic we must look we laugh, heads close together before he pulls me to my feet. We burst out laughing once we're balanced.

I launch onto my toes and plant a big kiss on his lips. How lucky am I to have found this? It might be from the sea air or the overexertion of running the full length of the ship twelve times, but I wouldn't trade any of these moments with him for anything.

Moving toward the stern we stop to order sandwiches and drinks from the poolside bar. We weave our way through the early afternoon crowd until we reach a free piece of deck space. We eat together and, afterward, we sit shoulder to shoulder, just enjoying more of each other's company in peace. Time passes so much differently out here. It's only when people start to trickle inside for dinner that Leo and I realize we've been out here for nearly four hours. It feels like we only ate our lunch minutes ago. I put my hand on my stomach, not hungry at all.

Leo pulls me up and chuckles. "You almost have to train yourself to eat more."

"I can understand why, I'm going to be twenty pounds heavier after this!" I laugh.

"And you'll be just as beautiful."

"Thank you," I say with a smile.

We take our full bellies toward the dining room, where the food will be too good not to eat.

The crazy thing is that, not too long ago, food was scarce for us. The things we ate during the war haunt me in my sleep sometimes, rotting vegetables and the fattiest meats you can think of made up our meals. Still, we were luckier than most. I don't want to punish myself for eating now, as much as my conscience begs me to scale back. The truth is, I might not ever have to feel hunger again. I might not ever have to worry about someone taking my home from me again.

Leo wraps an arm around me as we walk, shaking my thoughts of the past free from my head. I pick up my pace so I can walk stride for stride with him. As we return to the part of the ship we call home, we slow down, ready to enter as a couple. Tonight we will enjoy another fancy dinner together, and then later dance the night away with dozens of other lovers, before finally turning in for the best sleep we've ever had.

CHAPTER NINETEEN

Arden

September 7, 1940
London, England

"Look at Daddy!" Nora coos. She's sitting on the floor beside Klara, doing her best to put our daughter's attention on me. "Look at Daddy," she says again with her widest smile.

I'm met with bright round eyes and a perfect toothless smile. I kneel beside my girls and stack a few blocks in front of Klara. Her eyes widen as she reaches out for me. She has only recently learned how to sit up, and even so, Nora has a hand at her back.

"Your father makes a handsome soldier, wouldn't you say?" Nora asks as I gather Klara into my arms. I reach down and hoist Nora up beside us. She looks at me with the same eyes as our daughter.

I've never been the one with the looks, but to hear my wife call me dashing ignites a smile of my own. I steal a kiss, and then she brushes down my jacket. She'd laundered and pressed the uniform just this morning, wanting me to look my best for this afternoon's celebration. I'd been fast-tracked within the British Royal Navy basic training and quickly found myself in the Naval Intelligence Division. Lucrative and safer than most positions, I can't even begin to understand how I've been blessed with it.

"You're sure you won't come?" I ask, planting another kiss on Nora's head. I slowly pass Klara over. Nora's hand searches for mine, and I grip it tight as she needs both arms for the baby.

"I'd hate to go out and then have to turn right back around with her. We'll have a listen to the radio and turn in early."

Nora is introverted and quiet by nature, and the addition of Klara only lets her be more inclined to stay in the house.

"I won't be long," I say with one final kiss on the back of her hand. "Just a drink or two with the gentlemen and I'll be right home."

She chuckles. "Don't make promises you can't keep."

"I'll be home before bedtime." I blow kisses to my daughter and turn to the door of our apartment.

As I descend the stairs of our building and head outside past neighbors coming home for the day, I can't help but bite back the constant worry that's gnawing in the back of my head. I glance up at the sky and take a deep breath.

We'd fled Sweden with others when Germany had attacked Norway, that was only five months ago. Despite Nora's family begging us to come back, telling us Sweden would remain neutral and out of harm's way, Nora and I decided to stay in London. But day by day, it's looking better for Sweden and worse for England. Nora and I never speak about our mistakes, nor do we try to change things once we've set our minds to something. But with the dangers that continue to grow, perhaps we should rethink our way of doing things. With the sour taste of worry settling in my stomach, I try to force myself forward. As I round the block, the negativity fades. It's a night to celebrate something I never would have been able to back home.

I'm one of the last men to arrive. The get-together consists of other Swedish, Norwegian, and Finnish immigrants. Many of us have found our roles in the city that harbors us. Some found work in local shops or schools, while the majority found their path in the military. As the bell above the door signals a new arrival, I make way for them and migrate toward the boys in similar uniforms. I don't know them all, but there are still quite a few familiar faces.

The merry gathering consists of a few toasts, laughter, and overall happiness. I doubt I'll remember the specific details. Though I have a drink in my hand, I know my forgetfulness will not be due to the alcohol, but instead because of the way my mind wanders to my wife. Many of the men here brought their young wives or girlfriends. I think of my wife at home with our daughter. I can't remember the last time Nora and I went out and had any sort of time together. Of course, I wouldn't trade fatherhood for anything, but it would be nice to show off my treasure. As I take another drink, I promise to make time for us before my first assignment.

A few fellows pat me on the back and tell me good luck or congratulations, but for the most part, I'm left to my own devices. It's nearing four o'clock when I realize that no one would care if I left, no one would notice. Back home my girls are alone, noticing my absence every second. Beyond all that I miss them.

I'm halfway to the door when the bar slowly falls silent. The air is quickly overwhelmed by a cacophony of wailing air raid sirens and the sputtering sound of planes.

"What the hell is that?" Someone asks from beside me.

Planes. Planes intent on bombing us.

Chaos erupts as the whirring of engines grows closer. People dive beneath tables, others run for the stairs, and some decide to finish their drinks before moving for cover.

"Mate, what are you doing?" A man is looking up at me from his place beneath a table to my right. "Get down!" I stare at him, trying to figure out why the stranger would be taking interest in me. "Mate!" The man yells again. He grabs me by my leg and nearly causing me to trip. "You can't go out there!"

I hadn't realized my grip on the doorknob. I fully expected to go out the front door and sprint home. "My girls," I manage to breathe out.

"Nothing you can do for anyone out there!" He holds on tighter to my ankle. My heart is palpitating in my chest as I imagine Nora at home. God, please let them have gotten to the shelter.

The first bomb hits, shaking the dust from the rafters and splintering the windows facing the street. People scream and huddle closer together. I finally drop to the floor as a bomb lands down the street, shattering the glass windows. Inching my way toward a bench, I clutch at my ears, trying to block out the noise. As the planes pass over all I can do is pray. Pray that my wife and child are spared.

It feels as though the bombardment lasts an eternity, but as the all-clear is sounded, and I look at my wristwatch, I realize it's only been two hours. All around me, people are pulling themselves out of their spaces, stretching their limbs and haphazardly moving toward the door. Some men and women have tears in their eyes, though they are doing their best to hide them.

As soon as the first person opens the door to the street, the entire bar follows. Desperate to get to my family, I stumble out into the dying light of day and run. The pub's block is mostly intact, but as I move further east it gets worse. Entire buildings have been reduced to rubble, nothing but pebbles at my feet.

Families stumble from shelters, while others dig through the bricks of what used to be their homes.

When I turn the corner to my street, all emotion leaves me and I collapse to my knees.

CHAPTER TWENTY

Arden

July 21, 1956
MS Stockholm, Atlantic Ocean

The foghorn brings me out of my late-night stupor, as it always does. Panic ensues for a few moments before I can remind myself that I'm not in a bunker, or a pub, in London with planes flying overhead. Instead, I'm in my bunk, staring at the bulkhead. I release my death grip on my pillow and run a hand over my face. To calm down, I count the minutes, waiting for the horn to stop. As the siren continues to blare, I realize I'm not getting any more sleep.

Slipping my boots on and throwing a coat over my pajamas, I steal myself away from my room and head toward the deck. I join a few other men in a migration to see what the ruckus is all about. I'm glad it's working the way it's supposed to, but I'm angry that we would find the need for it at the tail end of the night.

It's no secret that the foghorn can evoke certain memories in people. Just a few months ago on an eastbound crossing, a young sailor had to be carted to the infirmary at the first sound of the siren. He suffered from what the professionals called, 'a gross stress reaction', but I know what he must have been seeing; it's what brings us all up to the top decks now. Horror stories, either lived or passed on, tell of the final moments of ships and their crews that now rest leagues below our decks. While we're not sinking, or at least I don't think we are, I'd rather be far above the water line on the boat deck than confined to the claustrophobic crew quarters.

When I emerge outside, I'm calmed immediately. The cool, damp air is invigorating, and it tempers the heat clinging to my skin. I'm able to take in my first unlabored breath as I step toward the closest railing. Nothing to trap me up here. It sure is foggy. Although it's not yet daybreak, the lights of the ship create a haunting glow all around. Turning out to sea, I raise my hand above my eyes to narrow my vision. I try to make out anything worth noting, but like my mates around me, I can't see anything, not even the water a few stories below.

As the foghorn continues to blast its rhythm, I move into the first-class dining room. I slouch in a leather chair near the exit and try to relax. There are only two passengers in the large room. A gentleman passed out over his glass at a table, and a young woman pacing close beside him. Perking up I study the pair.

"Is there anything I can do for you?" I state, hoisting myself from my seat. The woman looks me up and down before angling her necklace of pearls away. "It's okay, ma'am," I motion at my lapels displaying the crest of the company and the symbols of my lowly rank on my shoulders. She slowly turns back toward me and takes several steps forward.

"I just hope all this noise doesn't wake him up," she says, once again fiddling with her pearls as if I'll make a move to take them away at any moment. As if on cue, the horn blasts again.

"Perhaps we could get someone to help you back to your room? The sound might be more bearable there." The morning crew would be in soon, the last thing they would want to deal with before breakfast was two customers left over from the night before.

"Do you have the time?" she asks.

I look down where my watch rests, at least when I don't forget to put it on. "I do not. Though it's nearly sunrise, I think." Traveling west means running away from the sun. I have the body clock of a Rolex, until it comes to westbound crossings.

"You think? Aren't you a sailor?" she snaps, impatiently tapping her foot and crossing her arms.

"Yes, ma'am, I am."

She narrows her eyes at me and then turns away. Sitting back beside her companion, she rests a hand on his back and her head on his shoulder. She waits for several moments before speaking. "Lawrence, the horn has stopped," she whispers.

I realize she's right. With no care to hear how the rest of their conversation goes, I head back to the outside decks. Sure enough, the sun has started to clip its way in through the dying fog at our back. The path ahead is clear again, New York City lies somewhere just beyond, waiting for me to do what I should've done a long time ago.

I pat the pocket of my jacket, where my letter resides, and take a deep breath in and then out. I have yet to toss this one away. It's become comforting to have it sitting there, a cushion for me to pat when I feel the past trying to take over. Whenever I feel brave, I write a sentence or two at a time. It helps me to adjust to the huge task ahead, making it seem smaller.

Reaching for the letter, I pull it out and hold it up against the background of the horizon. Seeing it nearly complete gives me an overwhelming feeling of peace. It's a warmness I didn't know I could feel anymore. Looking up at the sky, I feel a presence beside me. Feeling inclined to speak to the presence, I bow my head. For the first time since the evening of September 7, 1940, I pray to God.

CHAPTER TWENTY-ONE

Adeline

July 22, 1956
New York City, United States of America

The phone rings twice before my mother picks up the phone. Newly installed, it takes her a moment to figure out how to use it, but soon I hear her voice. I hold the phone tighter to my ear and take a deep breath. Closing my eyes, I imagine I'm back at home in our living room after school having a conversation with her about my day. "Hi, Mom," I breathe.

"Darling," she begins. "I thought you'd never call."

"I've been busy with the girls is all."

There's one silent moment, but my mother refuses to skip a beat. "How is it all?"

"New York? Well, it's quite a change from —"

"No, that's not what I meant," she says.

I know what she meant. I curl a finger through the phone cord, willing her to come clean and ask me the questions I'm too afraid to answer unprovoked.

"Honey," she continues. "I don't want to beat around the bush, the last time I did that I lost you. So I'll ask you plainly: Are you happy?"

A part of me wants to desperately defend my decisions, tell her all is well, that Martin and I model a perfect marriage. As much as I want to play the part of a perfect housewife and lie through my perfected smile, I know she'll hear the truth in my voice. She is my mother after all, and she knows all even if she can't see me. "My girls make me happy, mom. I could be happy anywhere with them."

"Gosh, I miss them already." I can hear the questions in her voice again. Why'd you take my granddaughters? When will you be back?

"Martin promises we won't take such a large gap between our visits. Now that he has his footing in the company, he'll be able to take more time for us."

"Is that what you believe, truly?" Her question seems to pierce the façade I'm still attempting to maintain.

"Yes," I say in a strained breath.

"Adeline," she sighs. She's always been able to see right through me. Today is no different.

"No," I whisper. "I don't know." I let my eyes glance out into the busy lobby of our building before I lean as close as possible to the phone, as if every ear outside this glass box can hear me. "I've seen the old him this trip, Mom. He took us to Coney Island, and it felt like it did in the beginning."

"Well, you know how I feel about him." She sounded unconvinced.

"Mother please, just spell it out for me."

"You know how I feel about him. I won't bore you with advice on what I think you should do," she says, sounding defeated.

Before, she would tell me to leave him or say that I never should have married him, like she's done time and time again. But now it's different. I can hear it.

She continues. "I just want you to look at yourself, Adeline. Ask yourself what makes you happy and do whatever it takes to make it happen. You know if anything were to happen, you would be welcome back here with open arms."

Yes, open arms and a one-way ticket to the first bachelor still willing to have me. "All I want is for him to be present," I try to explain. "Not every second of every day, but enough for him to be able to tell when I'm upset, or to be there when the girls are sick."

"Well, he's more like your father than I thought. I should have gathered that with all the sulking he did on your visit."

My shoulders slump at the realization that she had also noticed his behavior. "He really is sorry about that. We're ... we're working through it."

There's a long pause, as if she is building up the courage to continue the conversation. "Adeline, I'm only going to ask you this once. I've held my tongue on the subject, but as your mother, I must ask. Do you feel trapped?"

The question burns through my stomach, into my throat, and out of my eyes. Trying to keep my voice level, I try to get out my answer, but I can't bring myself to.

"You've always needed adventure, Adeline," my mother says. "Always, since you were four years old and ran from the house to the barn in the middle of a storm to make sure Sue was okay."

A light laugh escapes my lips as I think back to our old mule Sue, the animal that lasted through the worst of the recession with us. I loved her.

She sighs, her voice softening. "I know I haven't been the most supportive of your match, but Adeline you have to know that I want it to work for you. I know the weight of marriage, and though I might not understand your decisions fully, I know you can bear whatever he throws your way. As much as I was against it for you in the beginning, we both have to remember that your story is a miracle. So many women would have begged for that opportunity after the war. Martin has brought you adventure beyond our small prairie farm. You've seen more of this world than I ever will. But above that, he brought your beautiful girls into the world to raise them with you. Be honest with him, if he truly is the man you say, then he will honor and respect your feelings, and he'll do anything to make it right."

A man steps up to the telephone booth. I look down at my watch as I realize my dime won't go much further. "I love you, Mom." It's all I can muster as my eyes begin to mist.

"Out of time already?" she asks.

"Out of time already," I echo.

"I love you, dear girl." There's a click and then silence. I hang up the phone with a shaky hand and step out of the booth. With my hands on my hips, I head toward the elevator.

She's right, of course. When have I ever been afraid of adventure? Of change? From chasing animals in a storm to moving across the world with a man I barely knew. When times get tough, I always try to remember the miracle she mentioned. I wasn't sure I'd ever see Martin again after we parted ways in March of 1945, but a few months later he showed up at my door, and with an address I never gave him in detail. I smile at the memory. My dad almost shot him, but when I told him who Martin was, he almost started crying, memories of his own time in France inevitably playing out in his head. This man and our children are in my life for a reason, and I can't take it for granted. We're allowed to struggle; I just have to be brave enough to confront it and work on it with him.

CHAPTER TWENTY-TWO

Eloisa

July 22, 1956
SS Andrea Doria, Atlantic Ocean

After attending Mass in the first-class dining room, Leo returns to his room to nurse a developing headache, while my family braves the upper decks with a few other timid families. I decide to take the time to explore by myself. I visit the Guido Gambone panels next door, and I'm overwhelmed once again by their beauty and the pure genius of the artist. I stand in front of them, gaping, until the lounge begins to fill up with passengers eager for brunch.

Slipping to the side I linger, wanting to enjoy the vision of the ceramics as long as possible. It's fun to be a fly on the wall, eavesdropping and learning about the lives of my fellow passengers. It's especially a treat to lean in on those traveling in first class. I snag a drink from a tray that looks like lemonade. After a swig, I realize it most certainly is not as innocent as it looks. I take it with me, sipping as I go.

Walking the length of the ship, I stop once I reach the lido deck. Below me, a cannonball contest comes to a close. They award a small kid the top prize, my guess is not for the biggest splash but for the biggest personality. He's hoisted on his father's shoulders, and he pumps his fists in the air as they take a victory lap in the pool. The happiness on this boat is infectious. I'm pulled into the standing ovation as the kid and his father exit the pool and the swimming resumes.

Having the urge to share this experience with my best friend, I ditch my drink and slip into the reading and writing room. Most of the cushioned seats are taken by people reading, so I move to an open desk. I cross my legs at the ankles and glance around the room, observing my fellow passengers. I recognize a young girl from our block of rooms among the many people enjoying their books. She looks up over her pages and offers me a smile. Leo told me that her name is Linda, and that her father is famous in America, that he has his own show on television. She seems normal enough, not as boisterous as Marjorie Baker or any of the American tourists that had trickled through Bari following the war. Realizing I'm still studying her, I give the shelves of books a once over. I never could force myself to enjoy a book, not when my brain can only tell a story in lines and colors.

Knowing that I've come to this room to give Anita a detailed story in my own words, I wince at the stack of parchment in front of me. Reaching for a blank postcard, I try to think of Anita and home, but my brain can only conjure the skyline of New York City. There goes the images, right on demand. My words once again fall flat. Flipping the postcard over, I find a colorful print of the Andrea Doria cutting through perfectly drawn ocean waves. On the back there are a few empty lines and a spot for postage. If Anita were sitting in front of me, holding my hands, I could bear my soul to her. But with a pen in hand now, I can only write a few meaningless sentences. Oh, how I wish I could tell her everything.

> *My dear sister, Anita:*
> *I hope you and your precious little family are doing well. I wish you could see the beauty of this ship and the sea. I find myself in awe of it each and every day I wake. Leo and my family say hello, we miss you and Bari very much. Now that New York is almost in sight, all of this finally feels real …*

My pen nearly runs right off the card and onto the table. It does all feel real, almost scarily so. Stretching out my fingers, I scrape my chair back from the table and run for the top deck, trying to escape the new-found pressure. I toss the note in the trash bin on the way out, it was worthless anyway.

Suddenly overwhelmed by it all, I have the urge to hug my mother. I've hardly seen her this voyage, and who's to say how much time I'll truly have to walk beside her when I'm married and start a family. Luckily there's a cool breeze today, so the heat of my frustration washes away quickly. I compose myself by smoothing down my hair and clearing my eyelashes of the accumulated moisture. As I start my walk toward the bow, it isn't long before I stumble across my family. For a few moments they don't notice me, and I see what they will look like once I leave them.

My father carries a smiling Gino on his shoulders, his rough, calloused fingers holding his son's squishy baby hands. My mother skips alongside my little sister, entertaining every single one of her questions and comments. I know I don't have many moments like this left, so I weave my way through the tourists and fall in stride with them. I don't make a comment to mark my arrival, nor do they. My mother merely smiles, and my father extends one arm and envelops me into half a hug. To some, it might look haphazard, but to me, it's more than I could ever dream of.

Our merry group continue down the veranda, a family that feels whole for the first time since before the bombs dropped on the harbor. I hold tight to my father's arm and imagine him walking me down the aisle in the next few weeks. I can feel the pinprick of tears in my eyes once more. This man had been my true best friend for years, and despite everything that he and I have gone through, I know that bond is still here somewhere.

CHAPTER TWENTY-THREE

Arden

July 23, 1956
New York City, United States of America

After all my time at sea, to say my legs are wobbly would be an understatement. A strange sense of relief washes over me as I topple to my knees at the bottom of our gangway. Erik comes up from behind and pulls me to my feet. If he finds it embarrassing, he doesn't make note of it. He gives me a curt nod and strolls onward with his mates. I lean against a wooden post as I force my legs to stop their wobbling.

We've finally found our destination, which I suppose is always bittersweet. Any passengers that you might make a connection with tend to slip away without a goodbye. This landing is no different. The Larsen family went on their way without incident, which of course I expect, but I would have loved to have hugged the kids once more before sending them on with their mother to their next adventure.

A thump from behind alerts me. "Well as I live and breathe," a familiar voice calls out.

Turning, I see Curt Dawe frozen to a spot on the dock, his crates at his feet. I raise my eyebrows as he comes closer. There are overflowing files of paperwork tucked under his arm. Out with the old and in with the new, I suppose.

"I don't think I've ever, and I mean ever, seen you off the ship." He pauses briefly before a kind smile spreads across his face. "It suits you."

I nod firmly. "103 crossings," I say, looking up at the steep bulkhead of the Stockholm. "Thought it might be time to see what the modern world looks like."

Dawe heaves a breathy laugh and then nudges my shoulder with his own. "I'm happy for you. Whatever you decide." I nod again and hardly have time to thank him before he's grabs his stack of boxes and heads for the Swedish American Line headquarters.

My feet finally remember how to walk on solid ground, and soon I'm off to God knows where. From here it doesn't look like the world has changed too much. Skyscrapers still touch the sky, women still wear pretty skirts, and men still bustle around the streets with their hats and jackets. Thankfully, I blend right in.

All along the streets are restaurants and carts with any cuisine you could imagine. Stopping at the nearest diner, I enjoy an American luncheon of fried chicken, corn, and sweet tea. It's enjoyable, but nothing beats the flavors of home.

The sun is no longer straight overhead, which causes the buildings hovering above me to cast long, dark shadows. As I pass by, I try to imagine them as ships. Perhaps in the future, they'll be that tall. They'll make floating cities someday, I suppose, and they'll be glorious. I can't escape the futuristic picture in my head as I go about my day. Meandering without purpose, I window shop and observe the melting pot of people. When I come across a little red post office on the corner of a block, I know what I have to do.

The letter in my pocket suddenly becomes heavy, and I clutch at it as if it were burning me. I can't remove it from my pocket fast enough. When I finally release it, I can't help but stare at it, unsure of what to do next. I thought it might mock me when I got to this moment, but here it is in my hand, nothing but a folded lined paper. A million thoughts flood my brain, but thankfully none of those beg me to toss it away. As if in a trance, I float up the stairs one at a time and enter the brick office. A bell tingles and I'm woken up, looking around it's just as one would imagine it to appear. Organized and full.

"Sir, may I help you?" A man in uniform makes his way from the back room. It would seem I've lost my words. "Sir?" he asks again, looking at me strangely.

I raise my folded letter in my hand. "I'd like to send this please." The man waits awkwardly behind the counter until I relax and move toward him. He stares at it.

"I'll get you an envelope and stamp for it. You'll have to put a name and address on it." He shuffles around for a moment and then lays the blank white slip in front of me. It doesn't hurt to write the name of my hometown down, in fact, it flows freely. I slide it back over to the man who immediately tries to slide it back.

"You've only written a town and a name here. No address?"

"It'll find its way," I say, stopping his advance. In a village of a mere 200 people, everyone will know exactly where it belongs.

I don't hear the man tell me the price, nor do I feel the coins leave my hand and hit the cold glass on the countertop. All I can see, hear, taste, and feel is warmth. The letter might only reach Sweden a day or two ahead of me, but at least it'll get there, at least there's no turning back now. What's done is done. My confidence leads me all the way back to the docks and up the stairs of my employer's offices.

The receptionist looks disappointed to see me. Only when I glance at the clock, do I realize it's probably the end of her day. "It'll only take a minute," I urge.

She takes her purse off her shoulder and sets it on the desk. With a sigh she says, "What can I help you with?"

"I'm putting in my resignation notice."

She doesn't ask questions about who I am, when I'm quitting, or which ship I sail on. She hands me a printed stack of paper on a clipboard and a pen. Questions she didn't care to ask verbally are printed on the sheets in basic type. The minutes tick away as I answer as thoroughly as I can. I have answers for every question, at least until the end. It reads: What is your reason for leaving? There's no box to check for righting wrongs, so I leave it blank.

I exit the building as a new man ... Perhaps not new, but rather have finally found my old self again. I'm practically buzzing with all the new possibilities as I make my way back to the Stockholm. Even at this hour, crewmen are busy refitting her with provisions and equipment for the trip back. Some early luggage has already arrived, and they're divided into groups in the entryway. A man organizing all of it asks for me to bring a suitcase from the door over to him, and I do so without question. There's no other conversation as we both go on our way. I'll miss the teamwork.

As soon as I get to my cabin, I pull on a sleep shirt and brush my teeth. It's early yet, but after such a busy day, it wouldn't hurt to try and get some shut-eye. Without the gentle rocking of open water to put me to sleep, I stare up at the ceiling and take in every crack and patched spot. I bang on the hull. "You've taken good care of me old girl. I'm honored to be taking this final voyage with you." With another less violent bang, I roll over and try to find sleep.

CHAPTER TWENTY-FOUR

Eloisa

July 24, 1956
SS Andrea Doria, Atlantic Ocean

"I told you!" Joanie claps her hands together and motions for me to twirl, which I do.

"Just like Audrey!" The other girls say in unison.

Joanie Baker had invited me to play shuffleboard with some other American girls this morning, and I was soon taken into their group. While the game was fun, the other girls spent most of the time telling me how much I looked like Audrey Hepburn in Roman Holiday. After they got over the fact that I have never once heard about the film, they dragged me to Sadie's room and pulled out a photo of the leads, explaining that it had been shot in Italy.

The picture had been bent in half to display the male lead, Gregory Peck, and had to be repeatedly smoothed out in order for Audrey to not become creased. When I refused the similarities, the girls went to work on me, pulling my hair back tight and going through Sadie's clothes for a new outfit. Now looking in the mirror, and after a twirl, I suppose I could see it in the cheekbones a bit. Holding my chin up higher, I pretend I'm a movie star surrounded by all my very best friends.

"We have to go show your beau!" Joanie says, clapping her hands again. The girls squeal and I'm swept up in the exodus out the door. Joanie links her arm in mine as the rest of the girls crowd behind us. I've never worn such expensive makeup or shoes before, but Sadie insists it is worth it, so I try to go along with her happy-go-lucky spirit.

We find Leo sitting at the open deck bar with a few other Italian men, including my father. His jaw drops when we make eye contact, and I blush. The girls nudge me forward and giggle amongst themselves.

"Ladies, you've brought me an absolute vision!" He sets his drink down and reaches his hand out to mine.

"What's this?" Papà asks, setting his cocktail down. I don't think anybody notices the darkness in his expression except for me.

"Looking like a Hollywood star!" Sadie says beaming.

"Go take that silly stuff off," Papà says.

"Papà —" I say with a deep breath. The comment has taken the girls aback; they're silent for the first time today. Leo's face falls, hiding his reaction. He grabs me by the arm gently at first, and then a little tighter when I refuse to budge. "We were just having a bit of fun," I try to say.

Joanie interrupts. "Sir, it was harmless. Please, it's just something that we do in the States for fun." My father turns on her, causing her to nearly run into him.

"Playing dress up as if you're children?" Joanie looks aghast. Her hurt eyes flick to me, pleading, but I merely drop my head in shame, there's nothing I can do to change his heart, so I let him drag me toward our cabins.

I hear Leo shuffling behind us, which brings me comfort. I know he won't do anything to intervene because I'm still my father's daughter, but I also know he will be there when I need him in the aftermath.

My mother is reading a magazine, Gino is nestled close, and Lucia is coloring when we enter. The peace is shattered when the door shuts and my father begins his scolding. "Just because you've been given this opportunity to go to America doesn't mean you get to act like those girls, all fun and games and not a care in the world." My mother sits up straight and studies me.

"Those girls are my friends," I argue. "It's not their fault they've grown up in a country that actually lets them be young women!"

"Young women?" He seems exasperated. "That's what you think it means to be a young woman?" He runs his hands through his hair. "You are going to be married in a few short weeks and you're galivanting around in another girl's clothes — a rich girl's clothes."

"She didn't mind. We were having fun, Papà! Why is that such a crime?" He grabs my arm as he did on the deck.

"No daughter of mine will behave in such a manner, regardless if they're in Italy, at sea, or in America. Do you hear me?"

"I'm not really your daughter much longer, am I?" I don't mean it, of course I don't, but his grip hurts, and if I stand here much longer I might burst in anger.

A cool hand rests where Papa still holds me. My mother's voice eases the tension. "Let's take a moment," she says as she situates herself between us.

His grip relaxes before he finally lets go and disappears out the door. I don't want him leave, but I don't want to look at him any longer either. I avert my gaze entirely, instead putting my focus on my mother. She smooths back a few unruly curls that have sprung from my ponytail, and then moves her cool palms to cup my cheeks.

"Darling, why don't you go clean up and return the clothes," she says in a soothing voice.

"I don't understand this," I say. "I don't know what I did wrong." Tears sting my eyes as I flee from her grasp and quickly exit their cabin.

Leo is waiting in front of my door. He has a look of concern on his face and his arms are crossed. I try to bolt past him. "I can't let you see me like this," I say, wiping black tears from my lashes.

"Yes, you can," he argues, hugging me from behind. I sink into him and let him hold me for a few moments. As people start making their way through the hallway toward the dining room for dinner, I finally break from our embrace.

My eyes are dry but still swollen, making me feel even more uncomfortable with being out in the open. Leo kisses me on the head and steers me into my room. "If you change out of your clothes quickly, I can run them up to Sadie's cabin."

"I don't want you to leave," I protest.

"Get comfortable and then meet me in my room. I'll take care of everything," he assures me. "Are you hungry?"

"Extremely."

"Good. In twenty minutes, meet me at my door." He kisses me once more and then shoos me toward my small washroom."

I give him an appreciative smile and shut the cabin door. I grab a comfortable slip and a dress before entering the small washroom. I briefly glance in the mirror above the sink; the dried mascara on my cheeks tells a story of defeat. I try to steer clear of dwelling too long on my reflection, but it's hard to do in the small space. It was only days ago that I had looked into the mirror at the hotel and felt like a woman, but after today, I feel like a child once again. I strip off the reminders of the afternoon and put on my starched, out-of-style dress. I fold up Sadie's clothes neatly and place the shoes on top. Dropping the reminders at the threshold of my cabin, I wait for Leo to leave with them before I return to the washroom and start to scrub the makeup off my face. I won't stop until I'm glowing pink and the tear stains are no longer recognizable.

Having lost track of time, I prepare to head straight to Leo's room. But as I reach the cabin door, I come out of my initial shock. The last thing I want is to see anyone in my family, so I peek my head out and run. Thankfully Leo answers on my second knock. As I step through the door, I'm overcome by what I see in front of me. Inside is an entire feast spread out on the spare bed, complete with two glasses of wine perfectly balanced on a ship's catalog. I also notice my drawings hanging on the bulkhead wall, which only causes my smile to grow.

"Not that you need them now, but your shoes are by the door."

He pulls me into a tight hug as the door closes behind me. After he holds me for a moment, I step away from the safety of his embrace. I rub my hands along his arms, trying to keep my composure. "How was Sadie?"

"Confused, I think." As he speaks, he absently runs his hand across his jaw. "She asked if you were okay and if you needed anything." He places a hand on my shoulder and steers me toward the foot of the bed.

"That's sweet of her." I say, bouncing slightly on the bed before coming to a rest. A sick sensation swirls in my stomach as I replay the reaction of my new-found friends. I bury my face in my hands and groan.

Leo's right hand kneads gentle circles in my back as he answers. "I told her I had it covered."

"I can see that," I say as I push myself back up. I try my best to put on a smile for him because I am so incredibly thankful for what he's done. "How'd you get all this down here?"

"Our steward was happy to help."

We eat our dinner huddled together on the small twin bed. It's the best dinner I've ever had. After the peach cobbler dessert, Leo moves the dishes to a cart in the corner and then returns. I lay my head on his chest and let him hold me close. My heart beats faster as I realize this is the first time we've ever been in a closed room like this together. I don't shy away from it like I might have yesterday. This man is my future, a future I am excited for and proud of. I won't be shamed by spending alone time with him.

After a long pause he asks, "Do you want to talk about today?"

I tilt my head up to look at him. "I've never seen Papà so disappointed in me."

"He had a few drinks before he saw you," he adds. Although it doesn't excuse my father's behavior, it does help explain things. Mother and I would occasionally find him with a bottle in the years after the war. He never became belligerent with his words or actions, at least not in the way he was today. His drinking seemed to decrease when Lucia was born and stop altogether when Gino came into the world.

I shake my head, shattering the memories of those dreary nights. "He's never like that. Never."

Leo hugs my head to him and takes in a sharp breath of air. "I'm sorry it happened."

"It's not your fault. I should have known he wouldn't have been pleased. We were looking for you, I just didn't expect him to be there," I explain.

"Well, we had quite a few things to talk about."

"Things that caused him to drink?" I ask, worry bubbling up in my chest.

Leo shrugs. "Things like a very nontraditional engagement and a wedding."

"I just wish my parents could see how things are in places beyond Bari. I know they are going through a lot, that they've given up a lot for me, I just thought they would be more open to Americans and their way of life." I nestle my head closer to his chest. He wraps an arm fully around me and we sit in silence for a moment.

"It's a lot to be open to," Leo finally whispers. "So many cultures smashed into one … To be honest, I thought it would be too much for you at first," he confesses.

"It is a lot. It's crazy how loud and confident they are, how the girls wear nicer clothes than my own best, but I'm ready. I'm ready to let go of Bari and Italy and the war and all of it."

He pushes me away from him slightly. "You can't mean that. What about Anita and the sunsets?" An evening years ago comes to mind. Anita and all our friends swimming at the beach once the oil from the bombs had finally dissipated and our beautiful clear water had broke through once again.

"I won't let go," he says. "I don't think I ever could; it's where I fell in love with you."

My heart melts at his confession. "I'm ready to move on with you." I slink my arms around him and squeeze hard. He tilts my chin up and holds it as he kisses me. I press into him and he into me. Finally alone, and finally able to explore each other without prying eyes. He treats me respectfully, never going too far, and never touching me without asking. It leaves me wishing the wedding was tomorrow.

Hours later, when our hands have stilled and our kisses have ceased, I lay awake. Leo lays next to me, his chest moving up and down with every breath. I snuggle closer to him and make the decision to stay. This is the only place I've ever been where I know I'll be safe and respected.

CHAPTER TWENTY-FIVE

Adeline

October 2, 1945
Lenexa, Kansas

On the farm, time is measured in cicada chirps and the squeaks of the windmill. With one leg tucked under me and the other hanging off the front porch railing, I look out over the fields. Father and a few of his farm hands are returning from a long day. It's the first full day of harvest after my return, and it is much duller than I remember.

I pull both legs to my chest and wrap my arms around them. A real fear of mine since returning is that I won't find enjoyment or a purpose in the quiet life here; so far, I haven't been proven wrong. 2,678,400 cicada chirps since my return and I have nothing to show for it, except the two marriage proposals I turned down and a job interview I was laughed out of.

My mother's voice interrupts my thoughts. "Adeline, would you mind coming in here to help me set the table?"

I take one more glance out at the fields before heading inside. Dinner is spread out on the kitchen countertop where it waits for me to move them to our dining room. I set the plates and utensils as the men trickle in from their day of work. Most wash up and head home to their own families, but two men join my father at our table. I try to keep a smile on my face as I pick through my food. None of the conversations, thankfully, are steered toward me. Tonight I retain my role of pretty accessory at the table; the silent and dutiful daughter.

Midway through the meal there's a knock on the door. My father scowls, agitated that someone would bother coming to the house at this hour. My mother, who has hardly had a chance to sit and eat, puts a smile on her face and smooths her dress. Thinking it's a field hand who forgot something, I continue to stare down at my plate, scooping corn back and forth.

There's muffled talking in the entryway, and then my mother reappears in the dining room pale as a sheet. "Mom, what is it?" I ask, hopping to my feet and laying a hand on her arm. She gives me an exasperated look at first, but then she quickly composes herself.

"It's for you, honey." She moves past me and sits beside my father, who has now become interested.

"Me?" I whisper, already halfway to the door.

The man stands on the edge of the porch, leaning against the same post I'd been sitting on an hour ago.

"Sir —" I begin.

He turns, and I nearly fall to my knees. Gripping the door frame, I step forward and he rushes to me, throwing his arms around my shoulders.

Martin.

When I pull away, he's crying. I wipe his tears and try to hold back my own. "Martin, how on earth —" I leave my sentence unfinished as I pull him back to me. He rests his head on my shoulder where he exhales a sigh of relief, as if he had held his breath for months. "How'd you find me?" I ask, pulling away again.

His hands linger on my arms as he answers. "You told me a farm in Lenexa, Kansas." His accent melts me from the core, oh how I have missed it. "I merely asked around the last few days." His hands leave my arms to shake back his hair.

"But why?"

A creak behind me reveals that my parents are listening within. Grabbing Martin's hand, I drag him out into the yard. He keeps up as we make our way to the barn. We stop just in front, right where my childhood tire swing hangs from the oak tree and an old rusted-out table sits in wait.

I turn back to him. "I'm sorry, I just had to get away from them."

"Your parents?"

"Yes," I smile lightly. He still hasn't taken his eyes off me. "I just don't think that the conversation we're about to have is any of their business, and I didn't think it was very appropriate to take you upstairs to my room."

He chuckles and the left side of his mouth curls up into the charming smile I remember in vivid detail.

"Adeline, *ma chérie,* I had to see you."

Suddenly my legs are wobbly, and I have to sit down. His strong arm guides me to settle on a nearby bench. "I never thought I'd see you again," I say with a little more hiss than I intended. We hadn't been much of anything to each other when we parted ways in France, or so I thought. I suppose we had been in love, plenty of people would have called it that, but any hope of continuing things had ended with an abrupt reassignment on his side and an end of a contract on mine.

"Things aren't the same back home. It's all so hard. Adeline, I have no one." My heart cracks in two when I catch his meaning. He had once spoken of a bright family, a lovely mother and two sisters. I don't have the heart to ask what happened, so I squeeze his hand and shoot up a quick prayer. "My whole town is gone."

A measly, "I am so sorry," is all I can muster. He squeezes my hand back and continues to share his piece.

"Adeline, I know our time was brief —"

"Is this a proposal, Martin?" I don't know if I can bear another proposal.

"I know it's crazy —"

I shoot up from my spot and cut him off again. "No, I can't. In the past month, I've turned down two men who I care for deeply. I can't in good conscience —"

"It's not a marriage proposal I offer, at least not yet. I'm sorry if that's what I insinuated."

"Oh," I say, flopping back down onto the bench. I fiddle with my fingers, upset that I could jump to such a conclusion.

Martin finally sits beside me and leans forward, his elbows on his thighs. "My village is flattened, but people are trickling back a few at a time. We're mostly holed up in a larger town just down the road, but there are so many that are sick or injured, some are my best mates."

"The Red Cross?"

"Isn't enough. I want you." What he's asking dawns on me.

"Even if I had the funds to go and help, I don't know if I'd even be allowed to," I say, crossing my arms and trying to find the logic in his request.

"You took an oath to serve," he argues.

"I did," I mutter. He looks around the farm at all the nothingness.

"You're wasted here."

"This is my home." I feel the urge to protest bubbling up as I look out at the rolling fields I've known my entire life, the fields I wished to see every day when I was at war.

Martin turns back to face me, taking my hands in his. "You said it yourself, you've turned down two proposals from men you like. You're not content here, you long for more."

He's right, but I'm not ready to admit it just yet. "I can't leave my parents again. It would kill them."

"Just come for a few months, help us get on track."

I pull away from his grasp, "Martin, I'm not in the army anymore, and I sure as hell don't have my own funds."

"Don't worry about that, Adeline. I traveled around the world, and when I got here, I visited nine farms before I found yours. I want you. I should've asked you the day I left, but I thought I'd be able to live without you. Don't fault me for that."

I glance back at the house. My father is holding his shotgun across his chest and my mother clutches his arm beside him. I lay my head on Martin's shoulder. I already know my answer, I knew it the moment he asked.

"In advance," I say, standing and extending my hand to him, "I'm sorry if my father shoots you."

"Good thing I have you to take care of me then." He tucks a stray piece of hair behind my ear before taking the lead back toward my parents — and what will be a very difficult conversation.

CHAPTER TWENTY-SIX

Adeline

July 25, 1956
New York City, United State of America

Sometimes I wonder why I have such a fascination with looking intently out of windows and staring into open spaces. These past few days have made me realize that it's not because I like the view, but because I'm looking out there for something new. That's what I was doing the day Martin tumbled back into my life, it's what I do now.

Juliet tugs on my skirt, curtailing all of my distressing thoughts. "Still in your jammies, darling?" I kneel down and smooth out her sleeves before picking her up and holding her to my hip.

Workmen had come early this morning, before the girls and I had even woken up, to haul off our luggage for the journey. Luckily Martin remembered to tell them to leave the day bags I'd packed. Pulling matching dresses and setting them on the bed, the three of us girls sit back and admire the look. I've purposely picked out outfits reminiscent of my own.

"Maman we match!" Johanna says, holding her dress to her body and swishing her skirt.

"Yes," I say with a smile.

Once they've changed and I've put their hair in braids, I sit back on my knees and hold their hands in mine, "Now girls, we are going to get on another big ship today."

"How big?" Juliet asks with wide eyes.

"As big as a city block," I say, accentuating my description by throwing my arms wide. "Which means we are all going to stay together." I point between our skirts. "We're matching so no one gets lost, and everyone can see that we belong together."

"Is daddy going to match?"

I try to find the words to let her down easily, but then Martin peeks his head in, and the girls turn their backs to me.

"What are you girls saying about me?" Martin says from the doorway. The girls run to him giggling. He picks them both up with ease and gives them each their own big hug. "Are we ready for our big adventure?"

"We're going home!" Juliet squeals to her sister. Martin gives me a questioning look, as if he's worried her usage of 'home' might stir up something in me. He's wrong though, the girls know France as their home, and I fully accept that. I only wish Martin could learn not to use my definition of 'home' against me.

"That's right honey," I say, pushing myself up. "We're going home." The girls wriggle from Martin's arms and then zoom toward the living room while laughing and speaking of France.

"I know today might be difficult for you," he says, reaching out for my hand. I take it and nod.

"A little," I lie. "This could never be yours or the girl's home, I know that."

"That doesn't have to change how you feel. You're allowed to feel upset about leaving."

"Martin, I promise you, I'm not upset. Anxious yes, but never upset." He holds me closer to him in an embrace.

"I'll do everything I can to make it easier on you."

"You won't forget about me and the girls on the voyage?" I feel him go rigid, but it's a question I have to ask. "You'll spend time with us?"

"I know I was distracted on the voyage over, and I know I never apologized for the way I behaved —"

"I don't need an apology. I just want to know that I'll be able to spend time with you, be able to talk to you, truly talk to you."

He holds me at arm's length and looks me straight in the eye. "I promise we'll talk. We'll have dinner and play games with the girls. We'll have a relaxing voyage as a family." He kisses me on the head, and I reluctantly melt back into him.

"You'll love the Île de France." His speech muffles in my hair, so I take a step back. I'd first heard about the ship during the war, it had been used to ferry prisoners from place to place. After, she carried thousands of troops home before it was put back in service as a luxurious steamship for passengers on the Atlantic. It's a piece of France that many locals, including Martin, love to discuss. To me, it's funny that a boat can become the pride of a nation, but perhaps my opinion on that will change in the next few days.

"I'm sure I will."

He sweeps my curled hair over my shoulder and traces the neckline of my blouse. "Is this new?"

"No." I laugh.

"Oh, well I like it."

His irresistible awkward humor is something I will always love about him no matter how hard I try. I plant one more kiss on his lips before evading his arms to find the kids. If today truly is a fresh start, then I want the girls to be with me for every second of it.

The girls are squished between Martin and I in our cab. They can hardly stay seated as the ships begins to come into view. They are no strangers to travel, but no form of it can capture their minds like the sleek bulkhead and towering funnels of a grand ocean liner.

Martin had shown them pictures earlier, and now that we're close they begin to play eye spy. Each time they think they've found the right ship they turn to Martin, who shakes his head and attempts to hide his smile. Finally, they come across it as our cab rolls to a stop. Juliet launches herself from her father's lap and toward my window. Both girls are pressed against it, craning their necks upward. Peering up myself, I can see why the ship is so popular. Imposing in just the right way.

The driver's door closing alerts me to get moving. Before I can open my own, Martin is there to escort all three of us out of the car. Holding little hands in both of his, we stand in contrast to the floating city in front of us. Even looking straight up I can hardly see the top of it. The ship we had come over on months earlier was nice, but nothing of this magnitude.

As a ship's official comes over to take our names and day bags, Martin gathers us up and steers us across the wooden planked pier to a beautiful glass building on the water. The inside reminds me of a grand train terminal, passengers mill about, and others sip on coffee or read the paper. Outside the Île de France sits and waits for her passengers to arrive. A man in uniform, touted to organize the meandering passengers, escorts us upstairs to a first-class lounge. Here we find a few empty chairs to relax on. The girls are given snacks and drinks, while Martin and I take to reading the magazines on the table in front of us. Perks of being early I suppose.

Despite the new issue of Women's Day magazine, my attention keeps getting dragged to the big windows in front of us that look out at the busy harbor. With so many ships of varying sizes, it's a wonder to me that they don't run into each other out there.

Realizing I've been staring out for too long, I turn back to my daughters and help them brush the crumbs from their dresses. All around me, good housewives tend to their children while sitting perfectly straight. Needing the reminder, I stop my slouching. Glancing around again I attempt to spy on the men. Some are chatting in packs, but the majority read their paper and sip coffee next to their wives, perfectly content. I've been confined to life with just my husband and children for so long that I forgot what society views as normal behavior for a husband.

Reaching over I pat his shoulder. Without missing a beat, he reaches over and traps my roaming hand. He plants a kiss on it and returns to his reading. I can feel myself blush, but as my eyes shift away, I catch another woman looking at me. She looks away as quickly as she can, but I saw her. I immediately fold my hands in my lap. I must remind myself not to be so hard on him, for others have it far worse than I.

CHAPTER TWENTY-SEVEN

Eloisa

July 25, 1956
SS Andrea Doria, Atlantic Ocean

When I wake before Leo, I'm torn between jumping up in a panic and quietly slipping out the door. If my parents found me here, they would be absolutely aghast. I'm sweating with nerves, expecting a knock at the door any second. I suck in a deep breath, along with all the fear. Glancing around the room, I try to figure out what to do through the haze left over from sleep.

Leo lays on the other bed, which he moved to late last night so as not to break any vows between us and God. In just a few weeks we'll be living together, and he'll never have to leave my bed again. He lays there peacefully; thankfully my rude awakening was not enough to disturb his heavy sleep.

Seeing my sketches on the wall where he affection-ately hung them calms me, and observing the tranquil space creates a need for me to capture it. I don't have my sketchbook, but I do have an unused napkin from last night's meal and an ink pen. Slipping across the small aisle between the beds, I sit beside him and draw. I always want to remember him like this; lips gently parted, hair ruffled in tight curls behind his ears, and his chest going up and down in even breaths.

In between glances at my work, I see his eyes flutter open. His mouth immediately curls up into a smile; he reaches for me before letting his tired arm flop down into the empty space next to him. His first thought isn't about what people will say, it's about why I'm not closer to him.

Setting my improvised drawing on the nightstand, I bend back into him as if he never left my side. He hugs me tightly. "I thought you might be gone when I woke up this morning," he says as his fingers run through my hair.

"I thought about it, but I'm happier here. Happier than I could be anywhere else." I let my eyes close as I completely melt into him.

"I love hearing that," he yawns.

"I love you," I say, forcing him to lock his arms around me tighter.

"I love you too." We sit for a moment, eyes closed, taking in the moment. His fingers tickle circles on the palm of my hand as we breathe each other in.

"What should we do today *amore mio*?" He asks after a bit.

"What haven't we done yet?" I laugh, thinking of everything we've crammed into our journey so far.

"Oh, a lifetime's worth."

"Well, we better get started then," I say, moving to the edge of the bed. I don't get far at all before he pulls me back to him and kisses me slowly.

"We've got plenty of time," he says against my lips. I kick my head back with a laugh but return to him in an instant, already missing his lips on mine.

My parents were at breakfast, but they didn't say a word to me. My mother gave me a smile in acknowledgment, but with my father still visibly upset, I knew she wouldn't dare say anything that would insinuate a return to normalcy between us. The only thing that got me through it was Leo holding my hand from beginning to end. It was still dreadfully uncomfortable, as I'm sure it was for everyone at the table.

After, we go for a lovely walk on the deck, which is rather crowded compared to our previous outings. It's a sunny morning, a normal morning. People sit by the pool, and others drink and laugh at the bars, all things we've come to recognize as routine here at sea.

As we come upon the shuffleboard courts we are thrown into a game with another couple, who we dominate. I celebrate when we win, and Leo spins me around in equal elation, but all that is brought down when Leo tells me the truth of the game. Apparently, shuffleboard is not something they play every day in America. It's a shame, I was hoping to sharpen my skills and enter a league. One of our opponents explains that the most important game is American football, which he tries to explain to us in detail. A boy who can't be much older than us produces a ball and a group proceeds to throw it back and forth for a while. My Leo is completely out of place, a man of grace with his feet, it's the other football he excels in.

He escapes that group as soon as he can to come over and wrap an arm around me. Giving me a quick kiss we both recline on deck chairs to take in the sun. We make chit-chat with a few other passengers for a while until we decide to head in for a late lunch.

As we make our way into the dining room, I can't get over how mundane the day looks from the outside. Luckily for me, I have this man beside who can make it feel like it's the most incredible day ever. I can't see myself ever complaining of boredom again if I'm with him. Smiling at the thought of forever, I squeeze his hand tighter because there is no way I ever want to lose this feeling of heart-pounding bliss.

My parents are no-shows at lunch, at least during the time we're there. Instead, we dine with another couple returning from their European honeymoon.

They're kind enough but too caught up in each other to pay us much attention. I can't say I blame them. I sometimes find myself too invested in Leo to care about what's going on around me.

CHAPTER TWENTY-EIGHT

Arden

July 25, 1956
MS Stockholm, Atlantic Ocean

New York is left behind as the Stockholm sails past the Statue of Liberty. The air has a sense of freedom to it, which I absorb until I feel chock-full of possibilities. Many passengers on this particular voyage traveling back to Sweden to visit family left behind, but for me, I'm finally going home. And this time I'm going to stay. I smile as we enter open water, watching the many ships coming and going in every direction. The difference between the majority of people and me is that they will more than likely have people waiting for them once we dock in a few days. I'll disembark on my own and wander home to a family who may or may not welcome me. Not wanting to scare myself, I shake it aside as the farewell crowd starts to disperse from the boat deck.

Catching up with a group of sailors, we make some final checks on the lifeboats and clean up a spill near the midship stairway. A few of the men shake my hand and wish me luck, the news of my leaving has evidently spread like wildfire. I'd like to think I've been a mainstay on this ship, a mentor to the new crewman throughout the years. While there's been a revolving door of other sailors, I've stayed. I pat the rail in front of me, summoning memories. Going on 104 crossings and never once has she given me a reason to doubt her.

"Excuse me?" I turn to find a young man and his wife. "Can you help us find our cabin?" My coworkers turn their backs, leaving me to help them.

"You might go find Mr. Dawe, our purser —"

"We know the number we just don't know how to get there," the young man hands me his ticket and I reluctantly lead the way."

"You're on D-deck near the stern," I explain.

"We're sorry to bother you," the woman says timidly. "It's our first time sailing." They mistake my silence for an invitation to keep talking. I don't mind, of course, I just like my quiet.

"You see, we've just gotten married, and my grandparents are in Sweden. I want to meet them before they pass." I turn and eye them, they must be in their twenties. Still, I say nothing.

"He'd like to see his homeland at least once," the wife adds.

"Where exactly is home?" I ask, holding a door for them to descend to B-deck.

"Minnesota," she says.

"Where in Sweden?" I clarify. The woman turns to her husband for his answer.

"Hässleholm," he answers.

I nod. "I know it.

"You've been?" His interest piqued.

"No, but my wife was born there."

"You're Swedish?" The wife asks excitedly. They truly don't know anything if they can't place me as a Swedish man.

"Yes ma'am. Born and raised."

"Well, isn't that fantastic Norman! You'll have to tell us more. As you can see, we are going into this a bit blind. My husband lost his parents last year in a car accident. They were going to go with us, lead the way so to speak …"

"I hardly know the language," the husband interrupts. "Anything you could tell us would be a great help."

My heart softens to this man's plight to discover his heritage, it's a luxury not everyone can afford these days. "I walk the deck every morning at 08:00 hours and every evening at 20:00. You can find me there and I will answer what questions I can."

The woman stops me in my tracks with a blossoming smile and a bone-crushing hug. "Thank you so much."

I grunt and give them a curt nod. We've reached D-deck. "Your cabin is just down this hallway on the right.

We part ways with handshakes and the nameless woman hugs me once more. As I turn on my heel and make for the stairs, her voice carries down the hall. "I told you God would lead the way. You just had to let him." I smile at the sentiment. Norman is a lucky man, some of the best advice a woman can give to a man is to be less stubborn and to let others take control sometimes. I wish I'd been given that advice at his age. I would have listened to people and made different decisions. I try to shake the possibilities from my head and think of how Nora would have never entertained the idea of mistakes ruining a day.

In her honor, I leave thoughts of past mistakes behind and make my way to Curt's office. He's most likely swamped, but on the off chance he's not busy, I'd like a word with him. Usually, on a day when we leave port, he has a line down the hallway, but with a half-capacity ship on this voyage, he has it under control. When I enter, he's filing paperwork, but he puts it down when he sees me.

"I heard this is your last trip, Lund."

"It's time to move on."

"Never thought I'd hear those words from your lips. I thought you'd be here until they put this ship out of service, or when you died, whichever came last."

We both laugh. Dawe pulls a bottle of whiskey from his cabinet. "You're not on duty are ya?"

"No, but I quit drinking." Dawe looks at me, stunned.

"You, Arden Lund, quit the bottle?" He sits back, arms crossed. "What happened to you in New York mate?"

"I sent a letter"

"I'm not going to even pretend to know what that means. A man's reasons are his own, I suppose." He pours a glass for himself and shelves the other while we sit and think about the past. Curt came aboard many years ago, like me, he's a part of this ship and her story. "I'm not going to pretend I won't miss you," he says, pouring another glass. "But that's as sappy as I'm going to get." I reach across the space and we shake hands.

CHAPTER TWENTY-NINE

Eloisa

July 25, 1956
SS Andrea Doria, Atlantic Ocean

"Leo, I will have a moment with my daughter now." My mother rarely poses her questions as statements, but when she does, you know you're about to be scolded. He looks between the two of us, but he respects my mother by leaving his seat vacant.

"I'll be by the pool," he squeezes my shoulder in support before descending the stairs to the lower deck.

"I want to talk about yesterday," she says, nervously shifting Gino from her chest to her hip. I pull my knees to my stomach and nod slowly. Taking the invitation, she sits down and faces me. I try to keep my focus on the strangers around me, hoping they will drown out my mother, but when she rests a hand on my arm, I have no choice but to respect her.

She inhales deeply before beginning. "I don't think it's a secret that all of this has been extremely hard on Papà and I …"

She's already fidgeting, tears swimming in her eyes. I quickly lose the battle as an angry daughter and reach forward to grab her hand, leaning in close so she can keep her voice at a whisper so as to not draw attention to her crying state. "I know it has," I say, rubbing her hand. I want her to know how much I love and care for her without saying it. I can't give in that quickly.

"I don't think you do, *mia figlia*. I think you think you do, but what you don't see is the effect it had on your father."

I sit up straight. "I saw it yesterday in full force."

"He thinks we've abandoned our home. Yesterday was too much for him. He thinks you've already forgotten what we went through as a family."

"Mamma, how could I forget such things? I was a child. I was alone and scared —"

"You had Leo," she corrects.

"This goes beyond that night, Mamma. The war was half of my childhood. As much as I would have loved the childhood you and Papà had running along the beaches and enjoying the Mediterranean Sea, I didn't stand a chance. Bari will always be home, but it will also always be the place where I almost lost both of you. Our own home is where I experienced the worst night of my life. No matter what, that is what will always pop into my head when I think of La Bacca Street."

"Please don't pretend all the times were bad." She looks hurt.

An echo of long-forgotten memories crashes into me: dancing in the kitchen with Anita, walking to the beach for the first time after the war ended, father buying the family its first radio — and how we listened to it for six hours straight on a Sunday afternoon after Mass.

Mamma eyes me but doesn't push any further. "You know your father is a proud man, he fought for five years, through the worst of it. Now that things are stable and we're leaving, he's beside himself with shame."

"Italy is your pride, but it isn't mine. Mamma, neither of you had to come."

"Oh, dear girl," she says, tears pricking her eyes again. "Of course we did."

"Why?" I say, indignant.

"When you have children, you'll understand."

Frustrated with the non-answer, I throw my hands up at the sky. "I don't know what you want me to do." I take her by the shoulders. "We are going to a new country Mamma, a new country with a new culture; we need to learn how to fit in!" Shocked by the rise in my voice, I fall back into my seat and cross my arms. "I'm sorry," I say, genuinely ashamed. When Gino starts to fuss, she instinctively stands up.

"I love you more than you know, darling." With a free hand she smooths my hair back and rests her hand on my cheek for a moment before turning away.

Letting my face drop into my hands in shame, my stomach turns and flips with the feeling of this unresolved fight. Soon those feelings are washed away by a soothing hand on my back. It rubs back and forth, gently coaxing me from my nightmare. Instinctively, I reach back and grab the hand, knowing it to be Leo's.

"How much did you hear?" I ask.

"Not much," he says, swooping down to sit beside me. "But I saw it all. I'm sorry for staring, I just wanted to keep an eye on you."

"What do you think I should do?"

"This isn't about what I think, Eloisa. What do you think you should do?"

"I don't know, that's why I was asking for your opinion," I scoff.

He scratches his jaw in thought for a moment. "I think you have time, so you should catch your wits and think through everything you're feeling. When you get yourself sorted out, then you should try and have another conversation with your mother, and if you're feeling brave talk to your father. Just make sure you keep calm and listen, truly listen. None of us are perfect, and even though I think you are perfect for me, I do know that sometimes your thoughts tend to wander during important conversations. I don't mind reeling you back in, but I don't think your father has the patience for that. He deserves respect from you even after what he did yesterday."

Of course he's right. He's always right. "I will, I just don't think I can today."

"That's understandable. Give yourselves time to cool down a bit."

"I will before the wedding," I say.

"Good." He pats me on the knee and then swivels around so he can sit right alongside me. He puts his arms behind his head, and I lay down, curling up on his chest. I let out the breath I'd been holding, allowing the sound of Leo's heartbeat calm me.

CHAPTER THIRTY

Adeline

July 25, 1956
SS Île de France, Atlantic Ocean

Sandwiches and sides are served at lunch. I wasn't expecting such a light meal for our first aboard the luxurious ocean liner, but Martin tells me that tonight's dinner will be extravagant.

We had come straight to the dining room after waving goodbye to the Statue of Liberty. Such a peculiar thing. Nothing has ever caused me to cry such tears of joy at one point in my life, and tears of dread and sorrow at another. It was the sign of peace I desperately needed upon returning home from war, and now it stands as the last bit of home I'll see in who knows how long. Martin had squeezed me tight, but I doubt he noticed the tears. The girls hardly noticed either, too busy waving at all the little boats we were passing by. When they're older they'll recognize the importance of the statue at sea, how she was a gift from their home to mine long ago.

The highlight of the afternoon has been the luncheon. By chance, we've been seated with one of the ship's doctors. He and Martin do much of the talking. Sticking to French, I join in where I can, but my input is mostly ignored. When the conversation switches to stories from the war, and Martin mentions I had been a nurse, the mood shifts and so does the language.

The doctor turns his attention my way and speaks in heavily accented English. "I hate to imagine a beautiful woman such as yourself amongst the mud and mire. May I ask where you were stationed?"

Surprised by a sudden invitation to the conversation, I have to clear my throat before speaking. "France, for most it. I was with the 12th Evacuation Hospital. We came into France after the invasion at Normandy and then moved around a lot after that."

"Ah, so you're American," I nod and take a sip of my champagne. "How on earth did you end up with this Frenchmen here," the doctor laughs and ribs my husband with his elbow.

"She saved my life," Martin says. My gaze finds his over the rim of my glass, and I'm forced to lower it. We both know I didn't save him from death, perhaps from loneliness or hopelessness, but not his life.

"Ah," the doctor says, rearranging his utensils. "I suppose that is all the reason in the world." Martin reaches across the table and takes my hand with a smile.

"You should have seen those American girls, Doc," Martin continues. "I don't know how they managed to look so put together all the time. We could be sitting in the rain with no cover and their hair would be perfect. Sleeping in the mud for a night? Perfectly tidy and put together. And they went through all of it for their boys."

I know it's hard for some people to believe, but we didn't do it just for the men around, we did it for our country, and to prove to ourselves we could. It had been months of walking, going wherever they needed us. I think the total came out to be eleven moves in the time that we were there. We gave up every ounce of comfort for our patients, and I know I would do it again in a heartbeat.

"Well, you know they could use you in Le Havre or Paris, wherever you're going," the doctor adds, looking directly at me. "They're in dreadful need of help in the clinics and hospitals."

Martin jumps in before I can even entertain the idea. "We're going to Montpellier for a few weeks and then we're off to Spain," he says, taking a sip of his champagne.

Sensing that he's in the middle of a tiff, the doctor's voice softens as he retreats behind his glass. "I'm sure they could use you there, too."

My heart ignites with possibilities, but upon seeing Martin's indignant expression, I return to role of dutiful wife. Smiling, I try to let the conversation come to a peaceful resolution. "That's very kind of you to think I might be of service, but —" I tuck my hair behind my ear, trying to think of an excuse, "My services are mostly used for bandaging skinned knees and dampening fevers of sick little girls." I was hoping to get a reaction from my daughters, but they are too distracted dissecting their sandwiches to pay any attention to the grown-ups having a conversation. "I wish I had the time for it." I take another sip of champagne and hope that someone changes the subject. No one does.

"Oh, I completely understand, a mother with a working husband. My wife knows the struggle all too well."

I give him a strained smile and then turn to my girls and attempt to clean them up. I'm relieved when I hear the men return to their conversation about the war in French, leaving me out of it.

We return to our first-class cabin after lunch. Martin sits down in our common space and pulls out the newspaper from this morning he had yet to finish. I'm tasked with putting the girls down for a nap. They go willingly, exhausted from their long adventurous morning. I have half a mind to lay down myself, but with Martin trapped here, I don't want to miss the opportunity to be alone with him. I join my husband, and as I recline against the armrest of his chair, he reaches back for my hand, and I give to him graciously. He kisses it and proceeds to give me secondhand news from the paper. I'm sure many women would be annoyed by it, but Martin used to do this all the time. In fact, he did it every day when I was pregnant with the girls, taking the time to tell me the lighthearted stories.

"Darling, come lay down with me," I say, tugging at him gently.

"You go on ahead, I'll be in shortly." I try not to let my shoulders slump with disappointment.

"Okay, I'll be waiting," I say with a quick brush against his lips and a swish of my hips. Both gestures go unnoticed.

"Oh darling, I almost forgot!" Martin adds, I've arranged to dine with the captain tonight, so we need to make sure we look our best."

"Captain de Beaudean?" I ask, turning from the doorway. "How on earth did you manage that?"

"Believe it or not, I know the guy. Crossed paths with him in '43."

"All right well, I'll bathe the girls before and dig through the luggage for something suitable."

"Thank you, my dear."

"Anything for you," I say, closing our bedroom door behind me. The smile instantly falls from my face as I kick my shoes off and drop my handbag to the floor. Constantly switching between being authentically happy and masking my disappointment is exhausting.

CHAPTER THIRTY-ONE

Arden

July 25, 1956
MS Stockholm, Atlantic Ocean

Just as New York had welcomed us with fog, she bids us farewell in the same manner. Visibility has been steadily dropping in the past hour or so. I've watched it slowly become thicker and thicker during the course of my evening route. Norman and his wife stopped by to say hello but didn't stay long, citing the weather and their adventurous nature. They bypassed me and headed straight for the dining room entertainment. Their choice to go off exploring instead of holding me hostage with questions suited me just fine.

I set my mind straight and finish my routine checks ahead of schedule. Distracted by the lack of visibility, I stroll up and down the boat deck as if I'm on the lookout. I'm fooling myself, acting like I'm working, when in reality I'm trying to take in every little detail of the ship. But despite my efforts to commit it to memory, I end up being distracted by all the new faces that pass me by. Sighing, I pat the rail and follow the influx of people taking refuge inside.

As soon as I reach the main dining room, I step to the side and lean against the wall. Stopping to listen for a moment, I cross my arms and take in the enchanting beauty of the moment. In all my years aboard, I've never enjoyed a meal in this room. There are probably a million experiences on this ship that I've missed out on, especially in these first-class rooms. I swallow the hard reality. If I can hardly fathom all the missed opportunities here, I can't imagine what I've missed on land.

Feeling my depression taking hold, I push myself away from the wall. I leave the liveliness of the glamorous room behind and go where I belong, outside with the creaking lifeboats and cheap deck chairs. Wanting to look back rather than ahead, I force my gaze forward and direct my route toward the stern. There isn't a soul around when I reach the very back of the ship. Rolling my shoulders to release a kink in my neck, I step up to a storage hold cap and sit down. For a long time I thought that there was nothing left for me if I did not have my girls with me, but now I've begun to realize that these thoughts were due to cowardice. There's a whole world of people out there that have lost things, in some cases have lost more than I have, and they fight for happiness every day. That's what I've finally decided to do, fight for happiness. There might still be a long road ahead of me, but I am finally ready to take that first step.

Peering over the railing in, I look down at the water below. The propellers churn the water, changing it from icy black to frothy white as we push our way through the Atlantic. As much as the sea can remind you that the world is vast and beautiful, it also has a way of reminding you how short life can be. I think that's part of the reason I came out here in the first place, to remind myself of that fact. I can waste away what little life I have left or find where the sea meets the shore and run toward forgiveness.

I try to imagine what my homecoming might look like. Nora's parents are well into their eighties now, and though they never once cast the blame on me, I know they resent me for taking their girl and their grandchild away the first time. I understand, as I resent myself too. They sent me letters throughout the years. Receiving those little envelopes with Sweden stamped on the front was never the worst part. The worst part was that I was selfish enough not to open them.

I rub my hands down my face, my stomach twisting with regret. There's nothing I can do about it now except pray that their hearts will be softened to me when they receive my letter. Maybe they'll toss it and turn me away when I reach their door, but for me to try and finally move on, I need to at least try. And try I will, in nine days. I just have to keep myself together until then.

Pushing myself up from my lonely seat, I stare once more over the stern and then shove my hands in my pockets. I'd consider Stockholm one of my oldest friends. She knows all my secrets and never fails to calm me. She always manages to do what I need of her. One more walk, I tell myself. One more walk, end to end, and your head will finally be clear.

I'm transported from one haze to another as I climb the stairs to the boat deck. The soft yellow lights of the ship reverberate off the thick fog, simultaneously suffocating me and making me feel warm, like the ship is in its own world.

I see Nora and Klara in the misty light.

Looking out to sea, Klara is older than I remember, standing on her own two feet and holding tight to Nora's hand. They both turn and smile at me.

A door slamming shut behind me bounces me out of the illusion. The water lapping against the hull hundreds of feet below helps ground me once again. No longer in another world, my daughter and wife are gone, replaced by strangers dancing in the haunting yellow light of the ship. I am left to wonder if they were even there at all.

CHAPTER THIRTY-TWO

Eloisa

July 25, 1956
SS Andrea Doria, Atlantic Ocean

I could get used to this. Leo dips me to the music, causing blood to rush to my head. Other couples move in sync all around, many brushing past us. It's a magical feeling to be in a room with a hundred strangers and still feel like you're one of two people in the entire world. It's even more magical when you realize you feel the way you do because your soulmate is holding you close.

I hope this is what marriage feels like.

Fragments of similar thoughts have been running rampant circles in my head all evening. With every lift and twirl, Leo and I become more in tune with each other's movements.

Over the past few days, I've become more confident with my dancing, and this evening we finally moved into the main ballroom from the surrounding outside decks. While I truly enjoyed the intimate setting outside, tonight it's almost too foggy to see either end of the ship. Besides, it's an absolute joy to be surrounded by other people our age. While there are some older folks, for the most part, it's teens and young adults with not a care in the world.

When the music changes to a slow number, Leo pulls me close and I lean into him, putting all my weight forward. He holds me there, hardly swaying at all. He's hugging me so tight I can barely breathe. Once I reciprocate, we stop moving completely, just caught up in our embrace. Other dancers do their best to steer clear of us, surely knowing this feeling themselves.

Overwhelmed by the abundant love overflowing the microscopic space between us, I pull back and slip my hand into my skirt pocket. In the middle of the dance floor, I pull out the sketch I drew while he was napping this afternoon. I'd rushed to put it away when he woke, so unfortunately it became crumpled in my pocket. I hadn't wanted to show it to him, but in this moment all I want to think about is marrying him, living with him, and spending the rest of my life with him. I hope he feels the same.

He doesn't say a word when he opens it, he just beams brighter than ever. On stage, the cymbals clash. Leo wastes no time, interlocking our fingers he grabs my hand and we run. I'm pulled along with him all while carrying the drawing as if it were glass. It contains my vision of us on our wedding day standing at the altar. Lace running rampant, flowers filling the aisle, my tea party length gown with lacey gloves to match, and his eyes looking into mine. It's what I envision, and even if our day doesn't match, it will be perfect as long as he is there.

We zip through the hallways, dodging passengers and crewmen alike. When we reach our hall Leo stops abruptly, causing me to nearly run into him. My parents are at their door staring at us. I immediately smooth out my dress and slow my pace to a walk. Leo squeezes my hand and continues, nodding to my parents as he passes by.

My father straightens, staring at me. He shakes his head and continues into their room. My mother visibly struggles with a long breath before reaching out her hand. I take it and she holds it there for a moment, not taking her eyes from mine. After a few moments, she breaks the gaze and pulls me to her. Ever loyal to her husband, she hugs me briefly and follows my father inside without a word.

I'm left alone standing in the hallway, her soothing touch still lingering. I flex my fingers, trying to rid myself of the feeling. I contemplate knocking on the door and having it out with them here and now, but as Leo said, there is time. I can speak with them when we're all ready to have an open and honest conversation. Why would I want to waste my evening arguing when I could be spending it with the one person on this planet who would never hurt me?

Dropping my head low, I stop at my door. I almost enter to say goodnight to Lucia, but I think better of it. Deciding to bypass it, I enter straight into Leo's room. He is facing away from me, his focus trained on a spot above the dresser. Alerted to the closing door, he cranes his neck, his arms lifted above his head, caught in the act. When he spots me, he lowers his arm and steps away to reveal my newest drawing tacked to a spot above his dresser. It brings the smallest smile to my face. Despite everything, he can still draw happiness out of me. He'll have to take them down tomorrow and might even be fined for all the little holes from his push pins, but there are no worries wasted on that, only on me.

"Are you okay?" he asks, admiring his work.

I nod, and like a moth to a flame I hover toward him. He runs his hands up and down my bare arms as if he were trying to save me from the cold. I feel him lean forward. "What's wrong?" I ask, turning to look at my drawing.

"Why is everything blurred slightly." He has good eyes. The blurring is so subtle that no one would notice unless they were this close and personal with it.

"It's not," I say with a laugh. "At least not everything. You're perfectly clear." I take a few steps back and sit on the bed. Resting my head in my hands, I let him know just what I'm thinking. "You're all I need," I say matter-of-factly.

His gorgeous, one-of-a-kind smile ignites on his face, and then suddenly his lips are on mine. I fall into his arms and somehow end up kneeling on the floor beside him.

"I can't wait to marry you." He entwines his fingers in mine and paints his picture of our wedding with words. Much like mine, his details are blurry, the only thing clear is us at the end of the aisle looking at each other. It's comforting to know that even with our youth we are both so certain about what the next chapter of life holds for us.

Someday, when my children ask me what being in love is, I will point to his exact moment and tell them. It's the feeling you get when someone you deeply care about rests their head against yours, caresses your cheek, and thanks God for your presence in their life.

CHAPTER THIRTY-THREE

Adeline

July 25, 1956
SS Île de France, Atlantic Ocean

It's hard to tell that we are even at sea aboard the Île de France. It's essentially a floating hotel, complete with a lavish party and highfalutin guests. The dining room has been transformed from the nice relaxing space it was at lunch to a lavish and glittering ballroom for dinner. Thankfully I was able to find outfits to match the occasion. The girls wear matching red dresses while I wear a golden, capped sleeve Dior gown. I purchased it in Paris last year but had yet to wear. I don't know what possessed me to drag it with me on this trip, but I'm glad I did because it has brought me to the center of attention.

I used to be quite the socialite in little Lenexa, Kansas, and even later in France when Martin and I took off. Of course, all that stopped when I became pregnant and had the girls, but I still enjoy a little champagne and glitter from time to time. Martin looks equally as dashing in his business tux. It's been a while since we've been the most stunning couple, but tonight it's as if we haven't missed a beat. We have two new little accessories with us to bolster us further as a picture-perfect family, from the outside at least.

Martin introduces me to a few men he knows by association, the girls run off to a corner with new friends, and I sip on my drink. Martin does well in keeping me on his arm. Many of the women I'm introduced to are wives, we make small talk and share understanding smiles when our husbands get too boisterous.

As the cocktail hour comes to a close, it gives way to a shuffling migration to tables throughout the room. As my girls sit at either side of me, I place their napkins on their laps, a service they are oblivious to. With such a fantastical world around them, their napkins are knocked to the floor in seconds. Instead of giving them a scolding, I grab two extras and tuck them into their dress collars. They're calm now, staring up at the main stage across the room.

Captain Baron Raoul de Beaudean's presence is met with a standing ovation. I've gathered that he is a very charismatic and respected man from the conversations held this evening, the sight of him does nothing to negate this. He stands at the microphone with a charming smirk and a stature that could make any woman swoon.

"On behalf of everyone here on the Île de France and the French Line, I welcome you aboard our beautiful ship of luxury. I hope you all have a wonderful evening and a fantastic voyage." Captain de Beaudean keeps his message short and sweet. He signals the band and descends the stairs and heads toward our table. When he reaches us and takes his seat, the dining room ignites with chatter and soft music. Waiters flood the floor, bringing appetizers and fresh drinks.

"How are we this fine evening Darbonne family?" Oozing with charm, he takes the tiniest sip of wine and relaxes back into his chair. I'm sure schmoozing guests is part of the job, but I still can't help but wonder about who exactly is captaining the ship on the bridge at this very moment.

"Very well Captain," I say, meeting his charm with my own. "We're so honored to have you at our table for the first course of the voyage."

"Well, when I noticed Martin on the manifest, I thought it was my old friend." He turns to my husband. "I thought I must've been wrong. The Martin I know? Married and with children?" The two men laugh, leaving me out of the joke.

To me there was Martin as a hardened soldier, and there was Martin as a partner, there was never a before for me.

"Friends?" I ask.

"The war, Adeline," Martin says from behind his rim.

"The war indeed, Mrs. Darbonne. But must we speak of it tonight? It's rather a downer topic." He says it as if I don't know the severity of the era.

"No, no sir of course not."

"My wife was a nurse," Martin adds.

"Oh, oh very good." He looks between me and my girls. "I suppose that's how he captured you then. Did he sweep you off your feet on the front lines?"

Martin reaches for my hand. "Actually, she swept me off mine." I smile in return.

"Well, you are a beautiful sight mademoiselle." He pauses briefly, sensing the conversation going nowhere. "Seeing that we all know the cruelties of the battlefield, we should sway the topic like we first intended, eh?"

I thought that the rest of the meal would be soured by the taboo conversation, but the entire table took it in stride, and we soon laugh the awkwardness away. Our oysters make for a delicious opening course and the wine is better than anything served in the States. Captain de Beaudean finds the time to compliment me and my girls on several occasions, sighting my wit and their humor as underrated qualities in women. It makes me realize how little Martin can find to compliment me about.

The aura around us changes drastically when the captain bids us goodnight and moves to his next table. The interactions between Martin and I become stilted, and our conversation turns stale. We might as well be on a first date.

It's not until the main course is cleared an hour later that I smile at something Martin says. In response, he takes my left hand and caresses my wedding ring. "You are stunning tonight, Adeline."

A pressure releases somewhere deep inside my chest, and I'm reminded why I fell in love with him in the first place. His innocent comment and calm demeanor are why I feel so safe with him. I'm about to reciprocate when Johanna lets out a frustrated groan and stretches out her limbs. It's a long time for anyone to sit still, let alone a child.

"I think I'll take the girls back to get ready for bed," I say, moving to leave.

Martin bolts upright, sending his chair backward. "I'll go with you."

"You don't want to stay for dessert?"

"I want to be with you," he says.

"You're sure?"

"Positive." He takes the lead, lifting a sleepy Johanna onto his hip. I grab Juliet's hand with my right and Martin's with my left.

Oh, how sweet it is to be purely happy with the person you love most, if even for a moment.

CHAPTER THIRTY-FOUR

Arden

July 25, 1956
MS Stockholm, Atlantic Ocean

Like a passenger thrown in a car accident, I'm launched from my bed and onto the floor. A chorus of singing sirens and blaring horns shake me to my core, while the accompaniment of a gnawing sound freezes me to the spot. In a dazed state between sleep and awake, I roll underneath my bed and wait. Moments later, I feel the engines reverse. We're moving again, but not without the whines and pops of metal being pulled away.

We must have hit something.

I hurriedly shove my pajama'd legs into my boots and run for the door. The engines have stopped, we're drifting now. Outside sailors run the hallway in both directions. Some toward the bow, but most scurry toward the stairway. Muffled voices cry for help, and I turn my attention toward them.

Fighting the gathering crowd, I reach an impasse. Where a hallway continued earlier today is now a knotted wall of iron. Men pull at the tangles, desperately trying to free a man just beyond the veil.

"Arden, it's no use here," Erik says, stepping away from the group. He grabs my arm and digs his heels in, trying to pull me in the other direction. "They need someone who can cut through all that. Who knows how safe it is down here anyway."

"Do you know what happened?" I ask, staring at the futile efforts in front of me.

He shakes his head. "No, I don't have a clue. I was finishing up my rounds and had my hand on the doorknob when the whole deck in front of me collapsed. When we reversed, the metal in front of me stayed. Whatever we pulled away from can't be faring well, and who knows what kind of shape we're in." Erik grabs me by the arm again and drags me with him.

"We'll come back with help!" he says over his shoulder, looking back at the man trapped at the wall and the men in front of him still desperately trying to pry the metal away.

We sprint down the hallway and up through the ship to the top deck. When we emerge, it's just as chaotic as it is below. Frightened passengers huddle in groups and call out to each other, part of the bow simply does not exist anymore, smashed in like a tin can. The scene is unlike anything I've ever seen.

A ghost white Captain Nordenson marching toward the boat house snaps me out of my trance. "Captain!" I call out. He looks exhausted, aged years since I last saw him a few days ago. "What happened?"

"I wa-I wasn't on the bridge." He stutters.

He continues his walk forward and I follow, not leaving without orders. Several officers approach him along with the ship's engineer. Thankfully, the fellow is able to relay that the Stockholm is not in immediate danger. A groan out at sea alerts all of us. For the first time, I look out over the railing. Out in the fog is a ship with her lights ablaze and a terrible hole gouged into her starboard side. The collision was only a few minutes ago, and she's already leaning well past a twenty-degree list. I can't get over the feeling that we have caused the accident.

I follow Nordenson into the wheelhouse where distraught Third Officer, Johan-Ernst Carstens-Johannsen, stands looking out over the mangled bow of the ship. He doesn't take his eyes off the ocean in front of us as he answers for the chaos. "We hit the Andrea Doria, sir."

Nordenson stiffens beside me, slamming his hands down on the windowsill before slowly gathering himself. "How did this happen?"

"The visibility was up to six miles. We didn't see them until it was too late." There are no further questions and no further answers.

The captain turns to me and waves over a man from the corner. "Go below deck and see if anyone needs help. Direct the passengers to get ready to receive survivors."

"Sir," the man says beside me. "Can we really take on a rescue operation like this?"

"We must, at least until others arrive."

The sailor nods in reluctant agreement and then flees.

"Sir," I begin. "I just came from below. There are people trapped. We'll need blow torches and jacks."

"Whatever you need."

A call to the engine room takes care of our equipment needs. Two welders meet me on the promenade deck, and we make our descent. I take one last look at the dying vessel. By the ever-growing tilt, I can guess she'll be gone by the morning. Thankfully, some of her lifeboats are already visible, slowly making their way down the side of a hull past the big black hole and into the water below. I offer up a prayer for the souls aboard and then run to catch up with the men in front of me.

We help the man stuck in my block of cabins, but the rest we discovered have already passed on. It's here I make the discovery that not all the casualties are from our ship. We pull out bodies, parts of bodies in some cases, that were clearly passengers of the Andrea Doria. When we are starting to lose hope that anyone else could be alive, we hear a voice clear as day, a girl's voice, speaking in a language I don't understand.

The men work fast to release the victim. She's fully conscious when we bring her out of the metal and onto the carpeted floor. I kneel beside her and notice how sickeningly twisted up her leg is. Broken for sure. "Get the goddamned doctor down here!" I call out.

When she speaks, her English is heavily accented, but she tries anyway. "I was on the Andrea Doria," she says, her eyes darting back and forth. "Where am I now?" No one has the heart to tell her. Two seconds later, she loses the battle with the pain and blacks out.

"Who is this miracle girl?" Someone asks.

At a complete loss for words, I can do nothing but reach for the girl's hand and hold it tight until the doctor arrives and relieves me.

CHAPTER THIRTY-FIVE

Eloisa

December 2, 1943
Bari, Italy

With my face pressed against the window, I look out over the harbor and try to imagine what Papà is doing out there now. I just know that I miss him. Sighing, I rest my cheek on the back of my hand and stare down at the street. Mamma is never this late. Throwing myself backward, I land on the cushions of our couch and stare up at the ceiling. I beat my feet against the soft feather pillows for a moment. Tired of being alone, I grab my dolly from the floor and toss her up above my head, over and over until I miss the catch.

When she hits the floor there's a slight jolt and then a massive crack. The whole building shakes for a moment before becoming still. Breathing heavily, I listen. There's another large boom and then the sound of planes. I peek out the window and see that the harbor is on fire. I watch as another ship goes up in flames, and then I grab the curtains and slam them closed. Grabbing my dolly from the floor, I run to our kitchen table and climb underneath it. Rocking back and forth, I try to block out the sounds but it's impossible.

Papà had told me that the planes were gone. The soldiers with shiny black boots had given way to soldiers with nice smiles who gave me chocolates. Confused, I clamp my hands down over my ears and pray for it to stop.

Despite the sounds of bombs going off, I hear the squeak of the front door. Leaping from my spot, I hope to find Mamma or Papà, but instead I find the boy from downstairs.

"Leo?" I ask, disappointed. "What are you doing here?"

He doesn't answer me. Instead, he grabs me by the hand and drags me from the apartment. I've seen Leo around the building and at Mass, and I know our parents are friends, but we've hardly ever even spoken to each other. Maybe he's alone tonight too.

I do my best to keep up with him as we sprint down the stairs. I trip once or twice, but both times he stops me from falling. When we make it to the main floor, I can hear the planes right overhead, but thankfully the explosions sound miles away. Maybe they don't want to bomb my house this time. Leo drags me into his apartment and leads me straight to the kitchen. He opens the cupboard door and helps me in. He tries to let go of my hand, but I won't let him.

"Where are you going?" I ask, willing to hold on for the rest of my life.

"I know where my mamma is, yours too. I'm going to go get them." He tries to pull away again, and again I hold firm.

"You can't go outside!" Just as I speak a bomb goes off, shaking the building's foundation. "They're getting closer."

Leo looks defeated. Reluctantly, he climbs in beside me and pulls the cabinet door shut. To fit comfortably, he has to put his arm around me, and we both have to pull our knees close.

I wince as the room shakes again. "Why did you come to find me?"

"I promised your papà I'd look out for you."

Leo and I try to count the minutes, but the explosions throw us off and so we give up. There's nothing for us to do but pray and hold each other tightly until the explosions finally stop.

Leo and I are barely awake when the cupboard doors are flung open. I squint my eyes, adjusting to the light and find Leo's mother staring at us. "Carlotta!" she cries. "I found them!"

I don't know how long it's been since the explosions ceased because there's still a deceitful ringing in my ears, but I do know that I'm safe now. I'm in my mother's arms, but I'm still holding tightly to Leo's hand.

Outside the world is burning, the bay is ablaze with orange, red, blue, and purple flames. The air smells like garlic, and it makes my eyes sting. Soldiers scurry about, helping my neighbors. A man tells us that all is well, that they won't be back tonight. I look up at my mother smiling, ready for her to be happy about the news, but she is looking out to the harbor. Her eyes glisten with tears.

"Mamma," I ask, tugging on her sleeve. "What's wrong?"

"Your papà," she says through her fear. I follow her gaze to the flames.

Mamma drags me all over Bari, Leo and his mother are never far behind. We search for my father everywhere. But as the sun peaks out over the water, casting light on the state of our town, mother finally collapses on a bench near our street. We'd gone as close to the harbor as the frowning soldiers would allow us, but our efforts went nowhere. But as my mother buries her face in her hands, my father limps up the street, a soldier on one side, Leo's father on the other. I jump from my mother's side, which gathers her attention.

We run together and crash into him. His leg is bandaged up from toes to mid-thigh, but he lifts me onto his hip anyway. His skin has the garlic smell, just like the air, but despite the way it makes my eyes water, I don't want him to let me go. He gathers my mother in and we hug, blessed to have been so lucky.

Next to me, Leo is having a similar reunion. I catch his eye and he smiles. There's something in the way he looks at me that I can't quite place, something that makes me feel dizzy. I smile back at him and think about all we've been through. After tonight, I know we'll be friends, perhaps more one day.

Luckily, most of the town did not have to suffer the wrath of German bombers. Our apartment is no worse for wear, aside from a few shelved items that rattled to the floor and one busted-out window in the kitchen. My father doesn't tell us much about what happened, just that an American ship was hit and unleashed something dangerous, which made the fire harder to put out.

It's not until I'm shipped off to my room for a nap that I hear him tell my mother what had actually happened. He explains that whatever had badly burned his leg also burned many other men, causing some to even to lose their sight. He insists that we shouldn't go outside until the harbor is clean and the smoke has dissipated. I watch through the crack in my door as Mamma wraps him in a big hug and whispers closely. For the first time in my life, I don't see my father hug her back. He pushes her away and then moves toward their room. She sits shocked for a moment before picking herself up and moving to the kitchen to start dinner.

I sulk over to my bed and fall face-first into the covers, exhausted I curl up and close my eyes. When

I can't get the vision of the harbor burning out of my head, I think of Leo's hand in mine and the feeling of his arm around me. The thought of him wards off the attempts by nightmares to overtake me, and I am able to peacefully find sleep.

CHAPTER THIRTY-SIX

Eloisa

July 25, 1956
SS Andrea Doria, Atlantic Ocean

A breeze whips hair across my face, tickling my nose. Swatting it out of the way my eyes slowly open. My vision is fuzzy and my head pounds, but despite the confusion, I reach out beside me for Leo. When my hand hits nothing but open air, I jolt out of the haze. Pulling myself from the floor, I rub the blur from my eyes.

Leo is gone. Leo's entire room is gone.

Letting out a scream, I kick my legs out, pushing myself away from the cliff in front of me. Pressing myself against the far wall — the only one intact — I heave air in and out of my lungs. Squeezing my eyes shut, I try to slow my breathing and calm down, but it's no use. My head throbs as metal groans and feet pound on the other side of the door. This has to be a nightmare.

"Leo?" I yell. I slowly pull myself to stand, but a wave of dizziness hits me and I keel over and throw up. A tearing pain rips through my head and causes my vision to go fuzzy. I wipe my mouth with the back of my hand. Coughing, I crawl toward the cliff. I don't know what I was expecting to find over the edge, but sure enough, peeking over I see the sea below me. Waves wash in and out just a few decks below, and the floor beneath my feet creaks with each rock of the ship. "Leo," I say again, except this one comes out a mere whisper.

The pain in my head is too strong to be a dream. I've never felt anything like this before, not even when I took a nosedive off my bike and hit a mailbox at the reckless age of eight and was deemed concussed.

My world is spinning. I don't know what has happened or how, but this is real. One moment I was sitting beside Leo at the foot of the bed, and in the next I was on the floor with the sound of horns blasting and the cold ocean wind slamming into me.

Tears spring from my eyes as I stare at the gaping hole in front of me. My stomach twists and I think that I might throw up again, but then the ship groans and rolls slightly. The fear that takes root in anyone who has ever sailed sprouts up in my throat,

The ship is sinking.

Tears still in my eyes, I claw up the wall and lean against it. There is one surviving drawing on the wall, so I tear it down and shove it into my pocket. It's a sketch of Leo's profile. If he is lost, if I never see him again, I'll need something of him to keep me going. I take a quick glance around the room for anything of his he might want me to take, but there's nothing else in the entire room worth saving. The only thing left intact besides the drawing in my pocket is the door and six feet of the floor in front of me. The door has been knocked off its frame, but thankfully, I'm able to get it open with a few hard shoves. People are running up and down the hall, and the ship's emergency lights are on, giving the scene an eerie red glow. Using the wall to brace myself I make my way toward my room where my sister is.

When I reach the doorway, I know it's no use. The door is splintered, bowed, and cracked. Trying to pry it open doesn't work, so I start to pull the wood panels back one by one. When I finally get enough pulled off to see inside, I find it in the same way as Leo's.

Gone.

Stumbling backward in disbelief, I feel my sister's loss hit me like a train. I feel like curling in on myself and waiting for fate to take me. I nearly do, backing into the hallway and against the far wall, I slide to the floor. Someone trips over me as they pass; they don't look back, just stumble forward before regaining their balance and sprinting forward.

The ship is sinking.

The ship is sinking and Leo is dead.

Lucia is dead.

I bury my face in my hands, hoping my own end will be swift.

Somewhere to my right, I hear a lone cry. I raise my head to listen. The hallway is empty but the cries continue.

Gino.

Scrambling to my feet once again, I can only think of my parents. Perhaps Lucia is with them. Yes, she must be with them. Whether I stumble forward due to the tilt of the deck or my lack of well-being, I'm unsure. I just know I need to get to my family. Fumbling with the keys, I'm able to get the door open with some force. Once inside I crumble to my knees. My father is hanging over the edge of the drop-off, trapped in twisted metal. I don't see my mother. Inching forward, I try to pull Papà back up but he's too heavy. I fall backward on my hands and stare at his lifeless body.

Gino has started screaming in his crib.

Gino.

Turning, I sprint to the corner. My brother lies crying in his crib, perfectly unharmed. It's only when I snatch him up and hug him to my cheek that I realize I'm bleeding. I do my best to wipe my blood from his face, but I've only smeared it. "My sweet boy," I whisper. "It's just you and me." With nothing left to do in this room, I run back into the hallway with my brother. Leo and I have taken this path many times in the past few days, and I'm extremely thankful because, even with the alarms and my earsplitting headache, I'm able to retrace the steps up to the top decks.

Despite the effort to corral passengers to their muster stations by an officer over a loudspeaker, the chaos has seeped onto the top decks. The ship is leaning heavily, which renders many of the lifeboats useless. A group of passengers is led past me by a man in a uniform. I fall in with the group. Gino's cries have ceased to a dull whimper, which I'm thankful for. I hold him tightly to me, trying to block out all of the uncertainties. I try to be strong for him, but the confusion and dizziness are slowly sneaking back into my head. I've made it up to the main deck, that should be enough. It has to be enough, for Gino's sake.

When the group shuffles to a stop on the starboard side, I reach up and tug on the sleeve of a woman in front of me. She turns and her face falls at the sight of me. "Ma'am, can you please tell me what's going on? I woke up in my cabin and my —" I can't tell the truth of it. "I'm confused is all."

The woman just stares at me, just as frightened and shocked as I am. She opens her mouth to answer but not before my knees go slack. The woman screams as I collapse to the deck. Gino is taken from me and replaced by gentle hands. Everything goes black around the edges as I watch my brother disappear with a woman into the crowd. There's nothing I can do for him now, he made it to the deck and those here will help him escape. His safety is the last thing I think of before blacking out.

I float in and out of consciousness as I'm carried to the promenade deck and swung out a window down to a lifeboat waiting in the water. Someone wraps a blanket tightly around me and another makes space so I can lie down. As we drift further from the Andrea Doria, a tremendous sorrow washes over me. I close my eyes again, not caring what happens next, but the woman caring for me encourages me to keep my eyes open. What's the point of listening to her?

I'm not sure how much time has passed when we reach another ship. She's nowhere near as big as the Andrea Doria and painted white. Perhaps this is the ship sent to take me to heaven. Perhaps Leo and my family are already there.

I learn that the ship is not a heavenly one all too quickly, in fact, it's the very ship that tore a hole into my room. I have half a mind to throw myself back into the sea as our boat is pulled up and out of the ocean, but I don't have the energy, so I let the passengers and crew help me onto the deck. An older white-haired sailor escorts us away from the edge and asks for our injured. I don't raise my hand, but the woman who cared for me in our lifeboat grabs me by the hand and leads me forward.

"I'm fine," I mumble, wanting to stay on the deck and watch every single survivor come in just in case God wants to grace me with a miracle.

"She's been going in and out of consciousness, and she has a cut on her forearm that needs stitches." I inspect my arm. I hadn't noticed it before, but there is a throbbing pain reverberating up and down it.

The man stares at me a moment before stepping forward and gently guiding me by the shoulder. There's nothing I can do, and as much as I don't want to go below deck on another ship, I know I need care. I let the strange man lead me down a shallow set of stairs and into an overflowing infirmary. The man makes no move to leave me, even as I'm given one of the only beds, even when the doctor evaluates me and promises to be back shortly. Neither of us speaks to the other, but I'm secretly glad for some company.

CHAPTER THIRTY-SEVEN

Adeline

July 25, 1956
SS Île de France, Atlantic Ocean

A glamorous night has dissolved into a dreary one in the blink of an eye. One moment we were telling the girls a bedtime story together, and in the next we were taking turns hitting each other where it hurts.

"In all honesty, I don't know where this is coming from, Adeline. I thought you were happy." The way Martin is looking at me you would think that I am a stranger to him, not his wife pouring out her heart.

I sigh, trying to think of my words carefully. "I am happy. I just don't think it's fair of you to ask me to give up a part of me that makes me feel whole."

"Are the girls and I not enough for you?"

"Of course you are!" I raise my voice. "You always have been, and you always will be. I'm just asking you to let me further my work in medicine. If my skills are wanted, needed even, then I should pursue it. If you are going to force me to go to a new country, again, then let me have something that will help me adjust."

"Force you? Last I checked no one forced you to follow me to France, no one forced you to marry me, in fact, I remember just about everyone being against it."

Stepping forward, I stand as tall as I can. "Tell me why you won't allow me to do it. When we shared our vows, you told me that you loved how adventurous I was, and that my courage and intelligence were the things you loved most about me. Tell me what changed?" He remains silent. I shove him lightly in the chest, pushing myself away from him. "Tell me to my face why you won't let me."

Suddenly, his face falls in shame and he takes a giant step back. "You'll find someone better," he says simply. "You'll leave me and the girls just like you left your home, except this time it won't be me you're following." There's a tense few seconds of silence as we both strategize how to continue.

"Do you even know me at all?" I say with a sad laugh. He looks to be near tears, and I am too, so I soften my voice and let the tension out of my fists. "I chose you for the rest of life's adventures ten years ago. I love you and the girls more than you will ever know. There is no scenario where I leave you. I vowed that I would always be yours, and you mine. You must have faith in me." I have an abrupt need to embrace him. We've never once expressed our emotions like this, but maybe if I'd spoken earlier, it wouldn't have gone this far. I'm simultaneously ashamed of myself and proud that I finally came forward.

He raises his head, honor and truth painted across his face. I can tell that the worst is over. Taking in a deep breath I collect him, his arms wrap around me tightly, and we breathe each other in. Despite the anger, his body is what I reach for when it's all said and done.

We stand embracing until Martin pulls away. I can tell that he's listening to something, or rather nothing, intently. "Have the engines stopped?" I ask, unable to hear the familiar hum that has become a comfort over the past few hours. As if the ship heard me, I feel them turn back on. We go to the porthole and watch as the horizon rotates with the turning of the ship. "We're turning around?" I say. "Do you think something's wrong?" I turn to my husband, who is already halfway to the door.

"I don't know, but I'll go find out." He grabs his jacket and opens the door to leave, but then he stops and returns for a quick kiss. "I'll be right back."

I nod and cross my arms, wondering what on earth we could be turning back for. I feel uneasy as he leaves. This could end up being a much longer night than I thought it would be.

While Martin is gone, I pace the room thinking of a million things that could be wrong with our ship, or perhaps even on the mainland. The ship doesn't shutter or lean in any specific way, which quiets some of my anxieties. Going back to our small porthole, I take note of the sea below, it seems that we are going at a much quicker speed than before.

The door bursts open and my husband appears, it looks like he's been running. "There's been an accident."

My stomach drops and a hand goes to my mouth, awaiting the news.

"An Italian ship and a Swedish ship collided back behind us. The captain has made the decision to turn around, apparently the situation is quite dire." I nod in understanding. "I saw the doctor on the way down," he says. "He asked if you would help. He has a few other volunteers lined up, but they are expecting to take on quite a few casualties."

I nod. "Of course." I immediately move to our room and change out of my gown into a plain dress. I pull my hair back into a bun, remove all of my jewelry, and dig through my luggage until I find my old boots I salvaged from home.

"Perhaps you should come with me Martin?" He stops his own transformation to look at me. "If they're truly expecting disaster, then perhaps it would be good if they had a soldier. All the sailors I've seen are so young, they wouldn't know how to handle such a scene."

"What would we do about the girls?" he asks.

"They're safer here than anywhere else, safer than the people we're about to rescue."

"I'll stay with them for now my love. I'm sure the crew is trained for this. You go and get things prepared. I'll come up if my assistance is required. For now, I'll try to get some extra blankets and make up some space for anyone who might need to stay with us."

"Okay," I say, slinging my bag over my shoulder.

I see a flicker of recognition in Martin's eyes. "You look ready to save an army."

I smile at his sweet comment. "Not this time."

"You'll be someone's saving grace tonight, just like you were mine." He kisses my hand.

"I hope nobody needs one," I say.

He kisses me then, slowly and thoroughly, like his most sincere apologies often are. "Well, you'll be there if somebody does." He escorts me from our room to the door where we share another kiss.

"Thank you," I say, squeezing his hand. As much as I wish he were coming with me to take on whatever it is we are cruising into, I know he will take care of the girls no matter what happens. I reluctantly let go of his hand. But knowing that we are okay, and that we have a better understanding of each other, gives me the hope I need to leave him behind.

Word has inevitably spread since Martin first discovered what happened. Despite the late hour, passengers have staked their claims on the upper decks looking out to sea, waiting to come across the wreck. If we were anywhere close, the crew would be clearing the onlookers and giving them instructions, but since they aren't, I suppose we have time.

When I arrive at the infirmary there are two doctors and quite a few nurses. Nobody questions my presence, instead, I'm handed a clean white overcoat and told we are expecting to receive patients with a range of injuries within the next two and a half hours.

We designate ten different zones in the small hospital, and each nurse is in charge of two beds, if you can call them beds. Clearly not equipped to handle an entire ship's manifest of injuries, the small medical team here has set up roll-away beds and a line of cots outside. There is no small talk, only preparation, which tells me I will be working alongside some very talented and professional individuals. Once the first patient comes in, I know I will lock in and be just as sharp and practiced as I was during the war. But until I'm called into action, it's big breaths and prayers.

CHAPTER THIRTY-EIGHT

Arden

September 8, 1940
London, England

I shuffle toward the crater where my home stood a few hours ago. A neighbor is calling my name, but I can't find it within myself to respond. Falling to my knees in the pile of smoking bricks I start digging, tossing one brick off the pile at a time. There is one story of the back left corner intact, but everything else has collapsed or been blown into the street. As people start to return from the shelters, a few more start to dig beside me, searching for their own belongings. I let my eyes dart up and down from my spot of work to the street, praying that they'll return to the surface with the flow of others.

Feet approach me and stop just within my line of sight. I look up at a shadowed figure, and I'm pleased to find a familiar face in the teacher from downstairs,

Miss Jane Lewis. Leaning back on my heels, I take her outstretched hand.

"Did you see my wife?" I ask, keeping all emotion that I can out of my voice.

"No Arden, I'm sorry. There was so little time." She tries to save herself by giving me hope. "Perhaps they went to another station."

"I need to make sure."

"Mr. Lund, I don't think that's a good idea. They'll be sending us help soon. It's best that we don't find them first."

"I need to make sure," I say, turning back to the rubble to claw deeper.

Jane drops to her knees in front of me and tries to swat my hands away. "If you find them then what? You don't need this on you."

She's kind, the teacher I'd hoped Klara would grow up to learn from, but she's unmarried and without children, she couldn't possibly understand. "If they are here, I need to find them."

She drops her hands to the debris like she's about to help but then the sirens start to blare. "Not again," she says, scouting the horizon to the east. Those all around me drop what they're doing and run back to the holes they crawled from earlier, but as far as I'm concerned, I will die here tonight.

Jane grabs my arm and pulls. "Arden, come on! There's still hope, you don't want it to end here. Not tonight."

"I'm staying here," I growl up at her.

I feel her release me but she's back in moments, this time with stronger hands. She and the volunteer she recruited haul me from the dent I've created and drag me down the street to the nearest tube station. I keep imagining we'll run into Nora and my daughter, but deep down I know the truth. Finally reaching the station two blocks away we clamor down the stairs with nearly a hundred others. I've regained my feet, but still my captors do not let me go out of fear I might bolt back above.

I don't sleep a wink, nobody does. The onslaught continues for hours, and as the day turns to night and back into a new day, somewhere in the haze of the tunnel everything changes. There is sadness, confusion, and above all hatred. When the sun comes up tomorrow, the British people will have the choice to lay down and roll over, or to bunker in for the fight of their lives, I would guess the latter.

It's 4:30 a.m. when we are finally given the all-clear. Some people are too rigid to move from their spots; everyone else is terrified but still marches up the stairs to meet the fear head-on. Jane and I choose to go up almost immediately. She has handled this extremely well for her young age. Never question the resolve of a young woman.

When we reach our street, we're thankful that it seems to have escaped the second round of bombs. As we step over the rubble of our home, we brace each other. My hands hover over the dig site unsure, but the chorus of ambulance sirens bolsters my resolve. They'll be too busy to look long, and I refuse to let a stranger carry them away from our home.

I know Jane has found them when she freezes next to me. She slowly backs away and lets me take over. I hear her sobbing as she turns and heads to the street.

They are laying underneath a fallen archway. Nora is holding Klara tightly to her chest. I take a deep breath to try and stave off the shaking, but it's no use. In disbelief, I fall to the ground and rest my arms on my knees. They're both a blueish tint, but they look unharmed beyond that. There is no blood, no oddly angled limbs, nothing but bruising that would suggest anything. Laying a hand on my wife's head, I push the hair back from her face.

Stuck in the repetition of stroking her head, it's not until Jane approaches with the volunteer ambulance drivers that I decide to continue moving them. I don't let anyone come near as I push the archway to the side and throw away each and every brick trapping them. I can't bear to look at my daughter as I lift them into my arms. Passing by the volunteers, they share their condolences and reach out their hands in prayer.

There's nothing I can say or do that will bring them back, nothing I can do to make it better. Lifting them gently into the back of a van with a dozen other bodies, I let my hands hover above them for a few moments, unsure of what to do. I had let them die alone, and I will never forgive myself for it. I give the driver my information and watch as they tag my wife and child before closing the door and starting the engine. Wiping my forehead with a shaking forearm, I watch the ambulance bump down the road.

Jane stands beside me, not even trying to hide her sadness. "You should go to the countryside," I say. "I'm guessing that last night was just the first in a —"

Jane puts her hand on my chest to cut me off. "London is my home. I'll not leave her or my students." She looks proud as she says it, proud and sure. She looks down the street where an army of ambulances are coming our way. "And what will you do?"

I'm still wearing my uniform from yesterday, though it could use a good wash and press, the important things are still visible. "I suppose I'm going to war."

She nods her head and doesn't try to persuade me to do otherwise.

CHAPTER THIRTY-NINE

Arden

July 26, 1956
MS Stockholm, Atlantic Ocean

One of the doctors left me in charge of the girl I escorted down. He says she needs an eye on her at all times, that she's severely concussed and there might even be damage to her brain. Every time she drifts to sleep, I keep track of her heart rate by gently resting a hand on her wrist and counting. I have no idea what this young woman has been through, but I'm not too worried about her pulling through. She wants to live; I see it every time she opens her dilated eyes.

The infirmary is busting at the seams, so I give up my chair for a man with a broken ankle. I hear that help is on the way, and that there are already some smaller ships taking on survivors of the Andrea Doria. It's better for me down here than up there. Keeping track of the well-being of one person is something I can compartmentalize. There are many crewmen from both our ship and the stricken one on deck coordinating the efforts and helping people. They don't need me, but this girl does.

Looking down at the girl, I can't help but wonder who she has looking for her. Nobody has inquired after her, not even the woman who guided her to me from their lifeboat. She's wearing a ring on her finger, whoever put it there must be worried sick. Hopefully her family is safe on a ship somewhere, but for now, it's just me looking out for her, and I take that role seriously.

A woman enters carrying a crying baby, which grabs the attention of everyone in the ward, even my patient. It's like she's pulled from sleep by a tow cable, shooting straight up and trying to get out of bed. I rest a forceful hand on her shoulder to keep her down. A nurse runs over. "Sweetie, you have to stay still."

Frightened, the girl's eyes jump to the woman and the baby. "I have a brother, a baby brother! I have to find him." I can tell she's about to break, so I take my hand off her and kneel down beside her. Eye to eye, I try to calm her.

"What's your name kiddo?"

Her struggling stops. "Eloisa Nicoletti."

"Eloisa, I'll go look for your brother, but you have to promise to do what the doctors tell you to do."

She nods ever so slightly and then settles back onto the pillow. The nurse eases her grip and turns to the next patient in need.

"Where did you see him last?" I ask.

"A woman took him from me on the Andrea Doria."

I pause for a moment. "There are a lot of rescue ships out there on the ocean right now, do you think he was in the same lifeboat as you."

"No," she whispers, "I don't know."

"What does your gut tell you?" She shuts her eyes and scrunches up the sheet in her fist.

"No," she cries. "I don't think he's here."

"Is there anyone else I should be looking out for?"

A darkness spreads across her face, there's no need for her to answer. Instead, I bow my head and hold her hand for just a moment, allowing a bit of strength to pass from me to her.

"I'll go look around." As I stand, the girl holds fast to my hand. "I'll be back I promise."

When she realizes she must let go, she gives it a frail squeeze and releases it. I turn on my heels and head out, averting my eyes when I pass a mangled young woman. I've seen enough of those in my lifetime.

Up top, the confusion continues. There's not much organization, aside from the goal of getting as many people off the sinking vessel as fast as possible. There are dozens of ships in the area, all with their lights shining brightly. Any captain brave enough to traverse the fog into a minefield of other vessels and lifeboats tonight deserves the highest honors when this is all over.

There are children everywhere but no babies to speak of. Little dots of people line the side of the capsizing ship, ship's lifeboats going up to the side one at a time to rescue more. This child could be anywhere. I'll do my best to search the Stockholm, but it's most likely they'll be reunited in New York when this whole mess is over.

My thoughts linger on the girl downstairs, on her face when I'd asked about other survivors. I shudder, knowing the look of loss far too well not to recognize it. To lose a family like this isn't much different than losing them to war. I think of my own girls before pocketing them and focusing on the task at hand.

Strolling the decks, I check in on groups of survivors and ask about the Nicoletti family. No one seems to know them or is too caught up in their own troubles to recall. I'm about to take the search elsewhere when all attention goes back out to sea. Shifting my gaze like everyone else, I see a floating city approaching.

One of the largest ships on the route, I recognize the Île de France almost immediately. Her presence instantly soothes me, with all her lights on it gives her the glow of a guardian angel. With the space to take on survivors, an experienced crew, and enough lifeboats to account for the ones lost on Andrea Doria, this rescue effort can finally be handed off to a capable crew on a ship that doesn't have its prow ripped off.

Bolstered by the news I return to the infirmary. Eloisa is sleeping but the staff is happy to hear that relief has arrived. They start to mobilize some patients for a transfer, but no one bothers me or the girl.

Realizing that no one is in need of services for the time being, I have a seat on the floor next to Eloisa's bed. Leaning against the wall, I tilt my head back and rest my eyes for a few moments, ready to wake if Eloisa should need anything. Leaving the site of a disaster can sometimes be the hardest part, we'll both need our strength to deal with that.

CHAPTER FORTY

July 26, 1956
SS Île de France, Atlantic Ocean

I'm outside sipping on a warm tea when the stricken vessel finally comes into view. The sea is a chessboard of ships and lifeboats zigzagging from one square to the next. I worry someone might hit us in this fog, but the engines are reduced to a dull hum and the captain demands that all our lights be turned on.

I had not experienced the horror of escaping a sinking vessel during the war, but I have friends who did. Images of what that must have been like are always in the back of my mind when I travel by sea, especially with my babies. Grasping the warm cup of tea in my hand, I get an eerie glance at the beautiful Andrea Doria on her side, succumbing to the sea inch by inch.

As the little boats turn toward us, I toss away my drink and return to my post. The first group of passengers are ailment free, but as the morning progresses, more crowd into our small infirmary. Luckily, most of the injuries are minor. We have a few head trauma cases as well as a few bones to set, but no one is critically hurt. I had expected a war zone, and I am forever grateful that it was not the case.

In between patients, I take a step outside for a breath of fresh air when a woman approaches me. "Excuse me, ma'am?"

"Are you injured?"

She shakes her head fervently. "I need you to take him." She pulls a swaddled cloth away from her chest and reveals a baby, which she passes to me. "I have to go find my family." She doesn't let me respond, but it doesn't matter because I'm already in love with him. Running back into the infirmary I console him, along with some of the nurses.

We come to the conclusion that the boy was saved from the stricken ship by a stranger, and that if he has anyone looking for him, they may not be on the Île de France. Someone procures a bottle and some milk, and the poor babe latches onto it and drinks the whole thing without putting it down. Once he's sound asleep, I strap him to my chest using an extra sheet from the linen closet. I continue my role as a nurse, and as my duties pile up my mind creates a story for the lost little guy at my breast. His mother must be absolutely frantic searching for him. I catch a cold shiver down my spine, thinking of what could have happened for a mother to be separated from her baby on a sinking ship.

I'm finally relieved after ten hours at my post. The last of the passengers, including the crew, were rescued from the Andrea Doria a few hours ago, and now we all sit and wait for the Andrea Doria to make her final plunge. She sits completely on her side, inching slowly down into the water. It won't be much longer now.

Martin found me a while ago and hasn't left my side since. Our stewardess offered to watch the girls until we are able to return. He didn't ask me for an explanation about the child, instead, he jumped in to help right away. He brought me breakfast and held the baby while I nibbled away on the buttered toast he procured.

Now we huddle close together near the rail with other onlookers. To my surprise, Martin is reluctant to give up the baby. "You've got to be exhausted," he says gently. He holds the baby tightly to his chest; he learned early on that this particular child does not like to be rocked.

When the time comes, I force myself to watch the Andrea Doria disappear. We had been watching her fight her fate for hours, and even now, as her stern begins to make its final plunge it glistens in the sun. The last bit of sun it will ever see. Holding tightly to Martin's arm we watch as the ship rolls once more and dips beneath the waves. There's a moment of silence and stillness, no one seems to know what to do, but then the engines rev and we are moving.

The Île de France circles the spot where she went down three times while the horn sounds, and then we point due west and are off at full speed. Martin holds me close, and then slowly but surely the crowd disperses, ready to start putting their lives back together.

On our way back to our suite, we escort several survivors to our hallway where our neighbors are ready to take them in. We take in a mother and her children who only speak Italian, and of course our little bundle of joy joins us as well. Juliet and Johanna are a bit confused about the whole ordeal. As a mother, what can I tell them about the death and destruction of the sea? Despite their lack of knowledge, they welcome our guests in with open hearts.

I'm able to give the mother a new set of clothes, but I don't have much to offer the young girls she's with as they are too old to fit the twins' clothes. My own girls sacrifice their beds and trudge into my room with their suitcases to move in. I escort the mother and daughters into their room. I pause just in case they might hint at needing anything, but they don't say a word, and so I close the door behind me.

Out in the main room, the girls are crowded around a freshly diapered baby. Martin stands above, arms crossed. "Girls, try not to crowd him," I say, placing a hand on each of them.

"Is he our new brother?" Juliet asks.

"I've always wanted a little sibling!" Johanna says, letting the boy grab her finger. I glance at Martin to gauge his reaction, but his focus is trained on the little one.

"Girls, we're going to take good care of this little guy until we find his mama in New York. Can you help me and your father with that?"

"New York?" Juliet asks.

"It's just for a few days, darling. There are some people we need to help get home."

Neither girl asks any more questions, their attention is already back on the boy. Figuring he's in good hands, I wave at my husband to follow me into our room. My hands are fraught with soreness, and they shake as I begin to speak. "Listen, I —"

Martin grabs my hands, stilling them. "You don't have to say a word. We'll stay as long as it takes."

I nod in relief. He knows exactly what I was going to ask. He kisses me on the forehead and caresses my knuckles. "You've been up more than twenty-four hours. Why don't you go to sleep? We'll be back later today, and we'll need your strength if we're going to find that baby's family. I can handle things out there for a while."

"I am rather tired," I mumble, trying to rub away an oncoming headache.

He pushes a stray strand of hair behind my ear and places his hand on my cheek. "Go rest, my dear." He wraps me up in a big embrace and then escorts me to the bed. He pushes back the covers and pulls off my shoes before tucking me in. He leaves me with one final kiss before the lights are turned off. I fall asleep almost instantly.

CHAPTER FORTY-ONE

Arden

July 26, 1956
MS Stockholm, Atlantic Ocean

I am reluctantly pulled away from the infirmary. I hadn't wanted to go, but there was a call for all hands on deck. By the time I arrive top side, the Andrea Doria is already gone, a minefield of debris left in her wake. The Île de France is sailing full steam toward New York, she's hardly a dot on the horizon now. The rest of the rescue ships have dispersed, save for a few United States Navy vessels that I assume are going to escort us back to the mainland. However, the issue is that we seem to be stuck in place. Evidently, the massive anchor chains on the bow were loosened in the collision, causing our anchors to slip and weigh us down. Chief Officer Källback leads a few volunteers in trying to break the massive chains with acetylene torches.

It's a nerve-racking task, and every man on duty stands as close as they dare as they keep trained eyes on the mangled bow where the chains are caught. A poor chap has volunteered to go over the side to reach a damaged portion. He hangs from a makeshift swing, dodging and dancing amongst the sharp edges of steel plating. We watch as he picks out artifacts as he goes, shoving them into his pockets. When he finds the main tangle, he pushes and pulls, finally freeing a portion of the chain after a few tugs. With the knot loosened, we pull the man back up from the wreckage and the fellas with torches begin burning the iron chains once again. After several tries, they are finally able to cut through the links. Despite the man's best efforts in detangling the mess, the chains do not fall free of the ship and into the sea as we had hoped, instead they stay in their place, clinging to the mangled mess of our bow. They continue to hang low in the sea, rendering us immobile.

Officer Källback leaves the site, clearly frustrated. As he enters the wheelhouse, we can see him and Captain Nordenson conversing through the windows. A few moments later there's a small lurch and a shudder as the crew above turns on the engines. I'm sure they're trying to use movement to free the chains, but as the Stockholm fights to sail forward, there is a terrible roar of tearing metal. Almost seventy feet of our bow, where it is still attached to the chains, breaks free and crashes into the sea. Everyone holds their breaths, waiting for the ship to slant forward with an intake of water, but it never does. In fact, it almost seems as if she settles backward without the weight of the mangled front half. Satisfied that the ship is safe, we finally leave the scene by rounding back toward New York, going at a slow and steady pace of eight knots. It'll take almost an entire extra day to get there going this slow, which means we'll also likely be the last of the rescue ships to arrive.

Fully intending to return to the girl in the infirmary, I figure I might stop at Dawe's office to write a report on Eloisa Nicoletti and her missing brother, but when I arrive, it is unavoidable chaos. The line grows bigger by the second as passengers make their way down from the upper decks. They'll all be trying to send in their names to shore. I would guess that half of those telegrams won't be sent to land by the time we reach New York. I do feel sorry for Mr. Dawe. He usually has such an easy time on these voyages, but he's completely overrun by emotional and frantic passengers, most of whom don't speak Swedish or English. I can safely say that I do not envy him in the slightest. Realizing that standing in the middle of the crowd is not going to help, I press myself against the wall and squeeze past the line until I can peel off into a quieter hallway.

A voyage that was half full last night is now overcrowded. There are people everywhere, some of the bigger cabins are now housing double the occupants. Thank God our voyage is short. I look up at the ceiling, tired specks floating across my vision. I do my best to rub them away, silently praying that the sea has no more in store for us. Tragedy is all around me, in the faces of every single person who passes by. Families huddle together, praying for their fortune, couples hold each other, and others weep.

In the infirmary, a whole other beast has emerged. People, mostly young adults, lay in beds with mangled limbs or head injuries. Never in all my years of sailing have I seen such carnage amongst victims of a shipwreck. As I dwell on the sequence of events, I think that we may have been the ones at fault. Sick to my stomach, I brace myself against the wall. The true number of casualties will inevitably come to light when we reach New York, but until then, all we can do is help those that have been thrust upon us. I get the feeling that my way of helping is caring for Eloisa.

Inside the infirmary, it's deathly quiet. In the corner, a white sheet covers a body. I put my hands deep in my pockets and watch as a priest prays over the deceased passenger. I turn and see Eloisa is awake, sitting up against her white pillows. She is watching the scene with tears in her eyes. As the prayers finish, she crosses herself and then acknowledges my presence.

"The man had a heart attack. I woke up as they were bringing him in here."

"Did you know him?" I ask.

She shrugs. "I recognized him." She shifts in her covers and looks me up and down. "Have you found anything out about my baby brother?"

"No, not yet. I'm sorry."

I notice that she is twirling her ring around on her finger. I can tell she already knows the fate of her significant other, she would have asked me to look for him if she didn't. Like me, I assume she didn't get the proper time to grieve or understand the loss before she was whisked away. It would be impossible for me to give her any sort of comfort, but I can at least let her know that she won't have to face the next couple of hours alone.

"I lost my wife during the war," I say, showing her my wedding ring. Her fidgeting stops and tears immediately well up in her eyes.

"He was already gone when I woke up. My sister and my parents …" She has to compose herself before continuing. "My brother is the only family I have left."

"We'll find him; he's probably on another ship." She still looks unsure. "Someone's taking care of him somewhere. There are an awful lot of good people in the world."

She looks at me for a minute and nods. "Yes, yes there are."

CHAPTER FORTY-TWO

Adeline

July 27, 1956
New York City, United States of America

Despite the early hour of our arrival in New York, the docks are jam-packed with reporters, safety officials, desperate families, and curious onlookers. The injured are the first to disembark, followed by Andrea Doria passengers, and finally it's our turn. Some passengers take everything with them and head to rebook passage immediately, while others leave some things aboard and find accommodation for the day. Unsure of what we are going to do, Martin has our things moved to a hotel a block away from the French Line offices.

I do my best to shield the baby as we push through the crowd. Reporters are still latching on to the lingering victims, some of whom stop and give brief statements. For the most part, passengers walk past, heads down and huddling with their families. If this is the firestorm now, the arrival of the ship at fault will cause a riot. We make it through the masses to the French Line quarters where we are stopped by a police officer. After showing proof of our passenger status, we are ushered inside. The lovely lobby is packed with passengers from the rescue ships and survivors from the Andrea Doria, but despite the crowd, there's a tired silence that permeates the room.

The entire morning, and the better half of our afternoon, are spent waiting to speak with an agent. By the time it's our turn, the girls have resorted to curling up on a nearby bench to rest their feet and are half asleep. The baby is wide awake, peeking out from his sling, he stares wide-eyed at all of those moving around him.

The woman at the desk looks exhausted, but she greets us with a warm smile. "How can I help you?" she asks, pen at the ready. With a firm hand on my lower back, Martin steps forward and takes control of the situation.

"My family and I were passengers on the Île de France —"

"Names?"

"It would be under Martin Darbonne."

"Are you looking to rebook with us, or can I help you look at refunding your trip?" she asks.

"We aren't here for that." He turns his head to me and gently nudges me forward. I pull down the cloth around the boy and tuck it into my folded arms.

I can tell by the look on the woman's face that she knows the child isn't ours. He doesn't resemble either one of us with his dark brown eyes, tan skin, and chocolate brown hair.

"Have you reported him to any officials yet?" she asks, pulling out a fresh piece of paper and jotting down notes.

I shake my head. "He was given to us by a passenger; she wasn't his mother."

"Do you have a name?"

"No," I say sadly. The woman makes a call and continues to write information down.

Next to us, a brilliant woman steps up with her family. She catches my attention instantly because, despite being caught up in the whirlwind of the past forty-eight hours, she is perfectly clean and put together. Her agent moves to the back room, so she leans back and ignites a cigarette from her purse. She notices my gaze and blows a puff.

"Mom," her daughter says in disbelief, stepping forward. "The baby." She reaches out for the boy's tiny hands, and I see tears of joy line her eyes.

The mother puts out her flame immediately and steps up next to her daughter. "Where'd you find him?" she asks.

"He was given to me by a passenger. Do you know who he is?" I ask, praying for an answer.

"We were staying just a few cabins down from his family. I thought —"

Her daughter finishes her comment, laying a gentle hand on her arm. "The ship cut right through their block of rooms; we didn't think any of them made it."

My heart leaps with the possibilities. "You knew them? Do you have names, numbers, addresses?"

"We spoke to the daughter quite a few times. Her name's Eloisa Nicoletti."

Our agent stands and finishes the last of her sheet. "I'll go check to see if her name has come through from any of the other ships."

By the grace of God, this woman happened upon us at this very moment. I pull the mother in for a hug and hold her there for a moment. "What's your name?" I ask, overcome with gratitude.

"Marjorie Baker."

"Thank you, Marjorie, we had no idea what we were going to do."

The daughter reaches up and caresses the baby's cheek with a smile on her face. "Eloisa and the rest of your family must be so worried about you."

Our little party is full of smiles, but when our agent returns the air changes.

"I'm sorry," she hands the paper to me. "An Eloisa has been accounted for on the Stockholm, but she's in their infirmary. I'm afraid that the rest of the family has yet to be recorded."

No one knows what to say. I hold the baby tight to me and kiss him softly on the head.

The woman reaches out and hands me the paper in her hand. "If you would sign this and put your information, we can contact you if anything changes." Martin puts down the number to our hotel, and Marjorie puts her arm around me.

"Eloisa is such a sweet girl. What on earth she did to deserve such a thing … She has a fiancé, they were coming to the States to start a new life, her family too."

"Poor thing," I say, looking over at Martin.

"We'll do everything we can to help her get settled," he says, rubbing the back of his neck, inevitably trying to put all the pieces together in his head.

Marjorie nods. "We're heading home to Georgia, but if you need anything, or if she needs anything, give us a call." She slips their number into my hand and holds it there for a moment.

"We will," I say. We part ways, none the wiser about each other's lives, but drawn together by the fate of one baby boy and his sister.

Outside the sun has already started to disappear behind skyscrapers. I carry the baby, and Martin carries two sleeping girls down the street.

When we check into the hotel, we all collapse onto the nearest beds. Our luggage is stacked in the corner, reminding me that this ordeal is far from over. With three sleeping kids between us on the bed, I roll to face Martin. "What are we going to do?"

He reaches across the space on the bed and pushes my ratted hair behind my ear. "We have to stay until we see this through."

"Can you spare that time?"

"It doesn't matter, we're not going to leave this child with anyone except his sister."

"If we can even find her."

"We will." Martin gently pushes himself up from his spot and comes around to my side of the bed. I roll onto my back to let the baby sleep on my chest. I wish I knew the sweet thing's name.

Martin leans down low to meet me. "I'll go back out and wait for the ship to return. I know they said they'd call us, but they'll be so busy, I'd hate for us to be forgotten."

"I should be the one to go," I whisper. Martin puts a firm hand on my chest, keeping me on the bed.

"No, it's getting dark out. I'd hate having you out there by yourself." I nod in agreement. He rests his hand on the boy's head. "Plus this *bébé* has had enough adventure to last a lifetime."

Martin kisses me and the girls before dousing the lights and slipping out the hotel room door. I hug the sleeping baby close and take turns running my hands through the girls' hair.

CHAPTER FORTY-THREE

Eloisa

July 27, 1956
New York City, United States of America

I was carried off the Andrea Doria on a gurney by Arden and three other men. It was humiliating to be carted out in front of hundreds of cameras and placed into an ambulance at the scene. The flashes caused my headache to return, and by the time we were halfway to the hospital, the bumpy ride had caused me to throw up what little lunch I had left in my stomach.

No one was waiting for me at the pier, and the same can be said at the hospital. I'd hoped someone had brought my brother, or perhaps Gino's family had found out I had survived. Realizing there might not be a single soul looking for me is a hard pill to swallow. If the only person left to remain strong for Leo is me, then all I have to do is keep myself breathing.

Once the doctor has gathered and written down my name and ailments, a nurse separates me from the other patients and wheels me into my own room on the second floor. A short nurse with mousy brown hair pokes me with a needle and connects me to an IV before leaving me alone. I hate the icy cold feel of the liquid running into my arm, so I stare out the window into the dreary city to distract myself. It's crazy that I used to picture New York with such a brilliant vibrancy, but all it has shown me since my arrival is a color scheme of gray and black. I doubt I'll ever be able to see the beauty in it after what I've been through. I break out in a sweat imagining what might happen to me now. Will I be shipped back to Italy? Will they let me stay? Will Leo's family still accept me? Is my brother somewhere safe?

Curling up on my side, I try to imagine him in the arms of someone kind, but the only person I can see is my mother. I have been so strong up to this point, so worried about everyone around me that I haven't had the chance for my emotions to burst. I didn't break down when I saw the bodies, or when I woke up on a strange vessel, nor did I cry when I discovered my brother was missing. It's here where I'm alone, surrounded by nothing but the shadows of my own memories until I finally cry.

Just when think I might pass out from the heat incurred from crying, there's a light knock on the door. I stop sniffling, but I don't bother to wipe the tears from my eyes when I call on them to enter. I simply don't care anymore. It's hard to care; it's hard to do anything but sit and stare at the wall in front of me.

The door creeks open and the guest hesitates before pushing it the rest of the way. Arden enters, his head low. "I don't want to bother you. I just want to make sure you're okay. They said you had a room, but they didn't know if anyone had come to get you yet."

"No, not yet," I say through leftover tears and a forced smile. Perhaps there's at least one person who cares about my well-being, an old sailor man I met yesterday in the least desirable circumstance.

He takes a step inside and cracks the door behind him. "I did some research on your brother, and I know for certain that he's alive."

I feel my heart stop. "Where is he?"

"That I don't know. A couple came in with him this morning when the Île de France arrived, but they couldn't give me names. They're working on getting them your information."

"Thank you, God," I say with a sigh of relief.

Frozen to the spot where he entered, Arden is still wearing his uniform from the first time I saw him. It occurs to me that he might not have anywhere to go. "You could sit with me for a while."

His eyes glance up at me from the floor. Without another invitation, he wanders over to the chair in the corner and sits down. I hardly know the man, but I do know that having Arden sit beside me adds a strange sense of calm I wouldn't have found otherwise. I think, perhaps, we both need each other right now. Neither of us has anything to say, and although we're both exhausted, I know it won't be a night where we're quick to find sleep.

After an hour of staring up at the ceiling, there's commotion out in the hallway. Arden and I both sit up a little straighter upon hearing the sound of high heels click against the floor and women's voices outside. They pause outside my room, and then a soft coo travels through the thin door. Arden stands, and my hand goes to my mouth as my heart beats faster and faster.

The door creaks open and a blonde woman with the softest smile steps through. In her arms is Gino, my Gino. My shaking arms shoot out toward him, and the woman rushes forward to place him in my arms. I snap him up, bringing him against me a little too harshly. I'm dousing him in my teardrops, but these are different than earlier. These are tears of relief, the sweetest I've ever felt.

The blonde woman sits at the edge of my bed smiling, her perfectly dainty hands resting on her lap. Arden has a hand running through his hair in disbelief.

"Thank you!" I say. "Thank you!"

"You're welcome," she says, shifting her weight and resting her hand on my arm. "He was a perfect angel baby." She looks away like she's thinking. "They never did tell me his name."

"Gino Nicoletti," I gurgle through a big kiss on his cheek.

Her smile brightens the room. "I'm Adeline." She doesn't wait for adoration or praise. "I know that you're here, and I heard about your family." Her grip tightens on me. "But my husband and I have decided to stay in town until all of this is sorted, so whenever they let you out of this place, we'll figure everything out, all right?"

I glance over at Arden, and he gives me one firm nod. I trust his input despite our short time knowing each other. "They're taking a better look at me tomorrow. The doctors on the Stockholm said I have a severe concussion." Adeline studies me and then nods in agreement.

"They'll release you soon then, you'll just have to take it easy."

"I don't know where I'll go." It's a plea for help. I don't want to sound desperate, but in truth I am.

"Oh, honey, don't worry about that. We'll figure it out." Something about the woman comforts me without end.

"You just focus on getting better." Arden hovers for a moment before heading for the door.

"You're leaving?" I ask.

"Just got some things to do kiddo." He sees my disappointment and then backtracks. "I'll come back in the morning. I think you're in good hands." Adeline nods to reassure us and then Arden dips his head in departure.

When the door closes, Adeline inches closer. "He's not family, is he?"

"No, that's Mr. Lund. He's a sailor on the Stockholm.'

"Please forgive my curious mind, but is there a reason he's helping you?"

I shrug. "He's just kind."

Adeline pats me on the hand, her touch is soft. She's a mother, I can tell. She pulls the blankets from my waist up to Gino's chin, covering us both. "Try and get some sleep. I can't promise I'll be here when you wake up, but I won't be too far away. I left my information with your nurse, so if anything happens, they'll contact me."

"You don't have to do this for me. I didn't do anything to deserve this, I mean, you took such good care of my brother."

"As you said, it's just kindness."

I ease back into the pillows as my brother nods off in my arms. With Adeline nearby, I feel as though I can finally try to find sleep. I peer down at Gino and start memorizing every part of his face, something I wish I had done before. I see my parents in him, I suppose I'll see them in him every time. He will undoubtedly be a constant reminder of what I've lost, and yet, I don't think I'll ever be able to take my eyes off him.

CHAPTER FORTY-FOUR

Adeline

July 31, 1956
New York City, United States of America

Eloisa and her brother were handed over to her fiancé's family this morning. I was ready to adopt
them both given the chance, but the moment that the
Marino family heard of Eloisa and Gino's survival,
they rushed to receive them.

Mrs. Marino had contacted Eloisa via a phone call
that was extremely hard on the young girl. I had to peel
her from the floor when I came to check on them. She
was sobbing. Although I was cautious of the family at
first, especially after the distress they caused Eloisa over
the phone, my fears were calmed once they arrived.

Arden and I had waited outside the small hotel
room the Italian Line had offered as reparation to
Eloisa. As the reunion took shape, our questions were
answered when both Mr. and Mrs. Marino gathered

Eloisa and Gino in a bone-crushing hug filled with love. While the sailor and I have little in common, we've both attached ourselves to the young woman, so we have no choice but to see her journey through.

The last few days have not been easy on any of us. As more information becomes available to the public about the sinking, the headlines become more and more troublesome. Both crews have come under fire for mishandling the events leading up to the crash, which Arden has taken personally. There's nothing I can do to soften the blow for him, but I've tried my best for Eloisa. I've kept the newspapers away from her the best I can, but she's curious and insists on reading them. It's rarely any heartening news.

Eloisa keeps all the clippings that she can find and puts them in a pile on the floor next to her bed. She never tells me flat out, but I think she's looking for confirmation from the bodies discovered. There have been a few recovered by passing vessels in the last few days, but no one that she knew.

Today's newspaper reported the death of a four-year-old who had been dropped on her head in a lifeboat during the hectic escape. She passed away in a hospital in Boston, never regaining consciousnesses. Another woman with a broken back is still in critical condition in the same hospital Eloisa was taken to. The only positive headline we've seen has been the story of Linda Morgan. They call her the miracle girl. She had been found in the wrecked bow of the Stockholm suffering moderate injuries. Her stepfather and younger half-sister had been killed, and her mother is grievously injured. Eloisa cried as she read it to me, and Arden confirmed the story, having been there when Linda was discovered by the crew of the Stockholm.

Arden hasn't been spared either. It's been confirmed that five of his crewmates passed due to the initial impact. There's a shadow cast over him, though I sense it was there before the crash. Despite the darkness, he's done his best to be there for Eloisa on her darkest days. He's assured me that he'll be around for a few more weeks so Eloisa will still have him after I leave. I'm regretful that I'll never get to truly get to know the man.

Now that Eloisa has been taken in, there's no sense in Martin and I staying. We've booked a crossing to France via the SS Liberté, the Île de France's running mate. I won't lie when I say that boarding a ship after everything has transpired scares me to death. There will be sleepless nights and nervous days aboard, but we have no choice. We've done what we can here, and it's time for us to move on.

"What are you thinking about?" Martin asks, coming up beside me.

I shake my head at the reflection of us in the window. "All of it."

Martin gathers me in his arms. "I know you said that you're ready to leave, but if you have any doubt about it, we can stay."

"Of course I have doubts. I want to wrap Eloisa and Gino up and keep them forever." I look back out the window at the funnels peeking out over the buildings near the shore. "When I spoke to Eloisa today, to say goodbye, I could tell she was terrified." I take a moment to consider where I'm going with this, "But I'm not saying we should stay. She's strong and has a family that will love her despite everything that has happened." A chill runs up my back thinking of Eloisa's reunion with her fiancé's family.

"How did the girl's family handle it."

"They were wrought with sadness, anger ... I don't think there are words to describe it." I look over at my children on the floor playing, imagining losing them makes me feel dizzy. "But they will love them both, that much was clear."

"And what of the sailor? Mr. Lund?"

"I don't know much about him, just that he promised me he'd keep an eye on Eloisa and Gino for a few more weeks. At least until they're comfortable."

"Poor fella, his whole livelihood's been put at stake. I mean, how do you return to sailing after your ship, your crewmates, are at fault for such a tragedy," Martin shakes his head.

"From what I've read, they're both at fault," I say, feeling oddly defensive of Mr. Lund and his crewmates.

Martin waves my comment away as if he doesn't have a stake in the tragedy at all. "It'll all come out in the investigation. If the insurance companies don't settle."

I cross my arms and think of all the passengers I cared for. "All those poor people," I shake my head. "They have to give them something."

From the look Martin is giving me, I can tell he doesn't think whatever is given out will be fair. "It's the way these things go."

"Well, they better be happy that I'm not in this country when the verdicts are read," I add.

"Ah, yes," Martin chuckles. "The ever-present protection of your patients."

"And what would you know of that?" I tease.

"I've experienced it firsthand," he smiles and kisses my cheek.

"I just want them to get the help that they need."

"So do I. There's only so much you can do, and you've done it. Eloisa and her brother are together because of you. Gino was taken care of and loved by you. All of those patients stuck in the infirmary after the wreck were comforted and kept healthy by you."

"I can't help wanting to do more," I say, wanting to have Eloisa and Gino in my arms. Itching to be of service again.

"I know," Martin says, reaching up and taking my hand in his. "You will, maybe not for them, but for others."

I hold him at arm's length. "What are you saying?"

"I'm saying, I think you should continue your practice when we get to Spain." He smiles at me, and I feel myself vibrate with shock.

"You're serious?" I croak.

"There's no way I could hold you back after everything I've seen the past few days. You could even continue your studies if you so desired."

I break through the veil of surprise and launch myself into his arms. "Oh, darling, thank you."

"You shouldn't thank me," he whispers in my ear before pulling back again, "I'm sorry it took me so long to realize this is something I should want for you. As much as I will hate sharing you, I can't be the one to starve the world of you, not when you have such a blazing talent and love for it."

Overwhelmingly happy, we embrace again. For the first time in months, I feel completely content in his arms. For the first time in years, there are no thoughts in the back of my mind telling me to wait or fight back. For the first time in forever, I know we will be okay.

CHAPTER FORTY-FIVE

Arden

August 15, 1956
New York City, United States of America

I feel as though my life has come to a standstill. I had it all figured out before the collision; I was finally ready to move on, ready to go home and discover my fate. I slouch back in my chair at the small kitchen table and rub my eyes. I hold the newspaper, whose front page has had me in its grasp for the last half an hour, at arm's length. The sailors I share this box with are playing cards on the bed shoved in the corner. They seem perfectly content in this limbo, but I've never been more uncomfortable.

We're playing a waiting game. Each and every one of us has put in our offers with the Swedish Line, which range from being transferred while waiting for the Stockholm to be repaired, to jumping ship and swimming toward other companies. I've thought about quitting altogether and sailing home as a passenger, but I need the money, and I think I'd go crazy with nothing to do but relax on a voyage. Our fates will be revealed when the Stockholm's running mate, MS Kungsholm, returns to New York. As the only direct line from the United States to Sweden, the Swedish Line has been playing catch up since the collision, running the Kungsholm and her crew to their limit. Luckily, they're finally starting to come out of it.

"Lund, stop looking at the stupid paper and come play a hand." Erik takes a long drag on his cigarette and stares down at his cards. His opponent hasn't said a word to me, or really anyone for that matter. His best mate was one of the five unfortunate souls to be taken in the crash.

"I would if I wasn't so busy," I joke, folding up the paper and tossing it across the table.

"Busy fretting?" Much to the chagrin of his partner, he puts his cards down and moves to the kitchen.

He pops open a beer and leans against the fridge. "All that matters is that we're getting paid."

I roll my eyes at his attitude and grumble, "Paid to do nothing."

Erik cocks his head to the side. "We've all been through hell brother. We did nothing wrong, in fact, I'd say that we bottom feeders acted perfectly dutiful this whole time. The least that they can do is pay us for the trauma that has been inflicted upon us."

While the papers had been harsh toward the leadership of both ships, it was noted several times that the crews acted valiantly in the aftermath.

Erik rounds the table and sits beside me when I don't answer. The fellow behind us lays back on the bed, staring up at the ceiling. We eye him sadly. "That's why we should be working," I whisper.

"Not everyone can drown out their past tragedies in work."

"It's still better than this," I counter, gesturing around our dilapidated flat.

"At least we have a spot to hold up. Some boys are camping out at the docks."

"All I know is that I can't sit here anymore."

As if the universe heard me, a knock comes from the door. I leave Erik at the table and open it, half expecting to run off some kids playing a joke. Our visitor is the furthest thing from a prankster kid. Curt Dawe stands before him, hat in his hands.

With some guilt, I take a look at Erik and close the door quickly behind me. I hate to leave him, but Curt usually brings news, and as I said, I can't sit inside any longer. I follow Curt through the dimly lit halls that have become home these past few days. Once we're outside, Curt puts his hands on his hips and stares up at the sky.

"All right Lund, what do I have to do to keep you around until the Stockholm gets put back into service?" He places a cigarette in his mouth and then hands me one. I don't like smoking much so I push it away.

"What have you heard?" I ask as he reluctantly puts my unlit cigarette back into his pocket.

"I heard you asked for an early release, and that they're going to let you."

"What about my housemates?" I ask.

"Haven't heard, more than likely they'll be taken home on the Kungsholm and then redistributed to other routes."

I nod in thought. "And what about you?"

"I asked to stay here until I can get back on the Stockholm. I have a little sway you know."

"That's because everybody likes you," I say with complete honesty. Curt huffs out a laugh and claps me on the back.

"They like you too. Come on Lund, you've been there longer than anyone, the only one to be on every single voyage. I think it's only right that you finish out your career aboard her."

I nod, thinking about the poetic justice of it all. "It's months away. I'm tired, and I'm ready to go home."

"What about that girl? I heard about how you helped her, we all have. Don't you think it would hurt her if you left so soon?"

My thoughts turn to Eloisa. Her family has entertained me for dinner a few nights since the sinking. I'd be lying if I said I didn't appreciate their company and kindness, but Eloisa is strong and already outgrowing anything I could give her. With Adeline gone, she has become much more independent, even attending church dances and going to stores with her brother. Her fiancé's family has taken her and her brother in as if they were their own without question.

"She's adapting. She sure as hell doesn't need me," I say, walking forward. I don't know where I'm walking to, but Curt follows.

"I wouldn't be so sure about that. You've dealt with a loss like this before. I imagine the weeks that followed were hell for you. A woman her age, I can almost guarantee she hasn't moved past it."

"She's pretty strong," I counter. "She has her brother and her fiancé's family."

"Her dead fiancé."

"What is it that you suppose I should do for her? I've done what I can. It's up to her to decide how she moves forward." I freeze in the middle of the sidewalk. I would stay with her if I could. "I'd spent so long not wanting to go home and then, when I finally worked through all my shit and was ready, it was torn away from me."

"And you're still ready to go home?"

"I'd like to think so."

"So write a letter to home and tell them what's happened. Hell, I'm sure they've heard about it all by now."

"Curt," I take a deep breath and turn to look my dear friend in the eye. "Is this conversation for the girl's well-being, or are you just trying to get me to end my career in a distinguished manner? What's your play here?"

"No play, I promise. I just don't want you to be hasty when you get called in tomorrow. If you value my friendship at all, know that I speak on behalf of the crew and myself when I say we would love it if you spent one more crossing with us. You are a part of that ship. We'd feel better if you were a part of her return to seaworthiness." Silence passes between us before Curt adds one final nail to the coffin. "Eloisa is very lucky that she had you looking out for her. I saw the families that were torn apart, and in some cases they had no one."

"Anyone would have done the same." I say gruffly, not wanting to think about it.

"Would they?" Curt puts a hand on my shoulder. "I didn't see anyone doing what you did."

He's right. But I didn't do it out of the kindness of my heart. I did it because I thought I'd be able to forgive myself for my own family if I helped save her. I wish I did it to be selfless, but I didn't.

I straighten up. "I can't promise that I'll stay, but I'll take what you've said to heart and think about it."

Curt pats me on the back before replacing his hat. "I'm glad to hear it. Regardless of your choice, don't leave without saying goodbye to me and the boys."

Curt gives a short little wave over his shoulder as he disappears back into the crowd of pedestrians. He has definitely made it harder for me, but maybe having difficult choices like this is a good thing.

CHAPTER FORTY-SIX

Eloisa

October 10, 1956
New York City, United States of America

I try my best to celebrate Leo's life every day. The home I now live in is filled with reminders of the love of my life. When I go to sleep every night and wake up every morning, I'm overwhelmed by the smell of him. I took Leo's room the day I arrived. Though I knew it would be hard, I needed a place to grieve, and a place where I could grieve comfortably without the eyes of others.

Of course, I share my room with my brother, and Mrs. Marino goes in from time to time to cry over his things. I suppose a few ghosts reside there as well; they tend to follow me wherever I go. I saw my father's shadow in the grocery line earlier this afternoon. It took a lot in me not to chase him. I know he's not there, it's just that I see them everywhere and it scares me.

Arden says the ghosts never really leave, that he still sees his occasionally. He tells me I'm lucky that it wasn't my fault, but I suppose he doesn't know that it is. We were all on that boat because of me. If I had been brave enough to go alone, it would've just been me, and we all could have escaped this fate.

The thoughts unsteady me, but I'm used to it at this point, so I press on. With a brown grocery sack in one arm and my baby brother in the other, I trudge through the streets of my new city. Though I believed the city was all shadows and dreariness when I first arrived, I know now there is indeed room for vibrant life. I might not see much of it now, but I know in time I will heal and the light will come back in full force.

I arrive back at the apartment to find it empty, which is not uncommon. Mr. Marino works as a plumber, while Mrs. Marino works at the department store just down the street. I don't think they know how to handle me just yet. I've known them my whole life, but they haven't seen me since they left Bari, and I'm not at all the same girl I was then. They've also lost their only son because of me. They've treated me and Gino as their own, but I know I can never replace their son, I know they blame me for his death.

Putting Leo down on his blanket in the sitting room, I move to the kitchen and put away the groceries. I like the monotony of the weekly grocery run and subsequent organization of the cupboards and pantry. When I don't have errands to run or chores to do, I sit on the couch and stare at the picture of Leo above their radio. The only thing that can ever wake me from my trance is Gino when he starts crying for me. It's no way to live, thus I busy myself the best that I can.

I check the watch on my wrist, noon. As I fall back onto the couch, I bounce my knee quickly, trying to hurry time along. Soon Arden will be here for our daily walk, and I won't be alone. I check my watch again and try to avoid Leo's eyes, though he's on every wall and shelf. I stare at Gino, who has successfully rolled onto his stomach and crawled toward me. His little arms kick out with each move forward, and his neck cranes up as he tries to find me. I smile to myself and kneel down beside him. When he gets tired, I help him sit backward on his bottom and reach for his new rattle, Adeline's parting gift for him.

The toy dips to the floor as I think of Adeline. I'm selfish in wishing she lived here in New York so I could talk to her whenever I needed. She was a mother to me for less than a month before she had to say her goodbyes. I didn't let her see me cry after she said her final farewell, though I suppose she's seen the tear stains on the letters I've sent her.

I stretch out my fingers, thinking of the next inevitable goodbye. I've told Arden many times these past few weeks that he can go on with his life, that nothing is holding him from Gino and I. He has refused to listen. I can only hope that soon he will listen and go where he's been longing to for so long. I just want him to be happy, and from what I can discern, that's not here.

Checking my watch again I know Arden will arrive any moment, so I hoist Gino up onto my hip. It's chillier than it has been, so I grab a blanket for Gino and a hand-me-down cardigan for myself. It was Adeline's parting gift to me, a deep navy cashmere button-up. Wrapping it tightly around me, I make it to the front door before Arden can knock twice.

The path we take is familiar. We walk a few blocks to the docks in silence, just absorbing the life of the city. Though Arden has never told me where exactly he is, judging from the way he can become overwhelmed by the crowds of New York, I expect he's come from a place a lot like Bari. We reach the Swedish Line headquarters, and he ushers me in. The first few days he brought me here, I couldn't bring myself to do anything but stare at the photos of the ship that killed my family, but as time went on, I learned to avoid them and focus on the task at hand.

There is a line of phone booths on the ground floor. While there are dozens on the path from the apartment and the docks, these are more private, and Arden demanded I get my fair shot at them when I want. Arden covers the fee and entertains Gino while I get twenty minutes for a call. It took a few weeks to set it up correctly so Anita could get to the right place at the right time, but now we talk every week.

The girl I left behind with her growing belly is due any day now. I stand at the receiver and wait as it buzzes. There is instant relief when she answers.

"Eloisa?" she asks.

"We don't have a little one yet?"

"Oh, it could happen any moment," she laughs. "If I leave abruptly, it means I'm off to the hospital."

"That close? You have someone there with you, right? Just in case?"

"Dino won't let me out of his site. He's pacing on the other side of the booth right now, fretting like a little mouse."

"And you're comfortable?" I ask, not wanting her to suffer on my account.

"No," she says with a chuckle. "I haven't been comfortable for weeks. At least here I have some company to take my mind off it."

I hear Dino's muffled voice come through the earpiece.

"Hello, Dino!" I call. "I'll only keep her for only a moment, I promise."

"He's gone," Anita says. "I know I talked to you three days ago, but I have to say it's nice to hear your voice, Eloisa. I'm still not used to not seeing you every day."

I choke back a cry. "I know I feel the same."

"Have you heard from Adeline lately?" she responds, changing the subject.

"Last thing I received from her was a letter saying they're getting ready to head to Spain."

"Such adventure."

I know Adeline isn't thrilled about it, but I entertain Anita anyway. "Yes, such adventure." Honestly, any mention of adventure these days has me running for cover. I wasn't always so afraid of living life, but can you blame me?

"How is Gino?"

I lean away from the phone to get a glance at him. "He's perfect." Arden is holding him, and a few receptionists have gathered around to play peek-a-boo.

"And Arden? Still confused about why he's stuck around?"

I hate talking about the man right behind his back, so I make my answer easy and honest. "I'm not confused. He made it clear to me the night we met that he has unresolved things in his past, I think him helping us is letting him heal."

"The world's business is just so callous these days."

She's expecting me to agree with her, but the truth is I don't. Bad things are always going to happen, but so are the good. "I know it looks that way, but you're about to be another little one's mama, and I ... I'm surviving."

"I didn't mean to come off unfeeling, Eloisa. I have a beautiful life. You are always welcome back here, please know that."

I don't have the heart to tell her that I will never be going back. I don't see how I ever could. It would be too painful. Gripping the phone, I bite my lip before letting her down easy with a lie. "I'll have to come to visit the baby. Maybe when Gino is a little bit older."

"Of course, whenever you feel ready." There's an awkward silence before Anita ends the conversation, "Eloisa, I should probably go. I love you so much, I hope you know that."

"I do." More than she'll ever know. "I love you too." I close my eyes and imagine us happily running down the cobblestone streets of home, Leo and Dino chasing at our heels. I'll never get that back, and though I know Anita and I will inevitably drift apart in the upcoming years, I want to prolong our sisterhood as long as I can.

I reluctantly hang up the phone. With my head downcast in thought, I exit the booth into the lobby. Arden and Gino are nowhere to be seen. It's normal for them to wander while I talk, but I still let my eyes dart around, trying to see where they might have ended up. A familiar receptionist catches my attention and points toward the front door with her pen.

I fluff my hair and pull my purse strap on my shoulder, ready to go back out into the real world. It's bright and sunny, and the fall colors of the trees are exploding in beauty. Perhaps I'll bring myself to draw again. I flex my hand as it cramps in want of a pencil, but I shake it free as I descend the steps to the sidewalk.

Arden hands me Gino, who I bundle up tight in the blanket. Arden and I begin the familiar walk back. He hardly ever talks, and today is no different. He's lost in thought, his arms clasped behind his back, eyes ahead.

When we meet our established corner of departure, he doesn't make a move to say goodbye. "Eloisa," he starts.

I pull a slipping Gino up on my hip. "Yes?"

He opens his mouth several times to say his piece, and eventually, he settles a hand on both of my shoulders. "You would be all right if I left, right?"

I rest my free hand on Arden's upper arm and look him deep in the eye. "Arden, we will be okay. It will be an adjustment, just like everything else has been, but we will survive."

He nods. "The Stockholm is due to start sea trials with the new bow soon, and then will return to her route."

"You'll finally be able to return home?"

"Yes."

I shove his arms away and wrap him up in a hug; he reciprocates briefly before stepping away. "You have to write to us at least once, that's all I ask," I say. Arden smiles lightly and nods again. I wipe my eyes. "Forgive me for crying, my friend. This is wonderful news for you."

"You're sure?" he asks again.

"Arden, there is nothing more you can do here for us. You have done so much for us. We can't ask you to stay any longer."

"I would stay if you asked," he says, head up high. "Just say the word."

"Then you understand why I can't. This was always meant to be my home, but I know you don't believe the same for yourself. You deserve to find your peace as much as anyone."

"Either way, I will miss your company."

I wish I could tell him that he reminds me of my father, but I think that might break both of us. "And I will miss you."

We embrace once more and then turn away from one other, heading toward our own apartments. I've endured a lot of hard goodbyes these past few days, but I have to keep reminding myself to be thankful for those opportunities. There is nothing I wouldn't do to have a hard goodbye with Leo, my parents, or my dear baby sister.

CHAPTER FORTY-SEVEN

Adeline

March 18, 1945
Trier, Germany

I nearly collapse when we reach the doorstep of our new hospital. With such a quick-moving front, we've marched around thirty miles from Luxembourg City to our new base in Trier, Germany. With the Nazis on the run, and the Allies taking the country mile by mile, we have no doubt that the war will be over soon. Despite this heartening news, it doesn't make our work any easier or less important.

After resting in the trampled grass for a few moments, I push myself and pull my bag along. The buildings we've been allotted are damaged in varying ways, but there have been around a hundred German prisoners assigned to the repair work. I try not to look at any of them as I head down the narrow street with a flood of other nurses looking to report. The Germans have been getting harder and harder to avoid as we push into their country. We've come across many of them, some we've had to treat as our own patients. Sadly, most of them are terrified teenagers who can't speak a lick of English.

There's not much I can do to comfort them except treat them to the best of my ability. Deep inside, I know it's not their fault, but after what I've seen in this war, it does nothing to make me want to advocate for them, even if they are young boys. It's something I hope to move on from when the war ends, but for now, my prejudices are my own.

When I get to my assigned bed, I drop off my things and sit for a few more moments. We're all so exhausted, and I can almost guarantee that they'll have us moving again in the next few days. The taste of victory in the air is what keeps us going at such a quick clip, that and the promise of new patients to care for. With the addition of prisoners, there's not much for us to do except check on our soldiers. Most will be trucked in as the days go on and the fighting intensifies further east. All around me, women take their time getting ready for the day. I have been with this group of ladies for over a year, and their persistence continues to inspire me.

We mill around, going ward to ward looking for men to help. A few need water, others bandages changed, but for the most part, the men are sorely in the need of conversation. Before the war, I thought of myself as a talker, someone who liked the attention on me because of my quick wit and sarcastic nature. Now, I strive to listen. Listening has become a way for me to relax. Entertaining via words is a tough task, while it takes nearly nothing to sit still and look pretty while a fella pours out his soul.

On the first break of my shift, I leave the stuffiness of the indoors and flee out into the sun. There's still a bit of winter chill, but a crisp breeze is always welcome when there is so much death and injury festering in the air. I have a seat on a crumbling stone wall and prop my feet up on a displaced block. All around me people work, talk, and live. It's enough to make a tired woman doze off, and I nearly do, but as I close my eyes, I hear feet shuffling near me.

My eyes dart open, and I'm ready to hop to my feet, but the man isn't a stranger intent on causing harm. The man is my own guardian angel; a man who has found me time after time and has yet to share his secrets.

Martin Darbonne.

"I should say that I'm surprised to see you, but I think I've finally realized that I shouldn't be." I reach my hand out to him, and he pulls me to my feet. We embrace like old friends, a warm spark igniting in my chest. He pulls away all too quickly.

I notice a young German staring at us, longing in his eyes. I'd seen it before, boys yearning for their sweethearts back home. I look away quickly enough,

Martin spies him and yells in German. The boy looks away and continues his work digging.

"How can you stand having them work beside you?" Martin asks. He looks from prisoner to prisoner, disgusted.

I shrug. "They don't bother us, if they did they'd be killed. They're just trying to make it to the end of this like everyone else."

I can tell there's more he wants to say, but he leaves the topic alone after heaving a deep breath. "It took me a few days to find you this time. The last letter I received made it sound like you'd be in Luxembourg."

"We were, for a while anyway. The war's moving, so we have to try our best to keep up."

"Understandable."

"And what about you? Care to divulge any of your secrets today, or have you come to whisk me away?"

Martin does not reciprocate my beaming smile, instead, he hangs his head low. "I didn't come here to exchange pleasantries." He has a serious look on his face for the first time since I met him.

I take a deep breath and prepare myself for the worst. Suddenly, the idea of losing him hurts me. I hadn't felt the need to worry about him throughout the whole bloody war, but if he's come here in person to break off whatever it is we are, I don't know how I'll handle it.

"I had to come and let you know that I've been discharged and am going home."

Whatever I was expecting, it wasn't that. "That's … that's wonderful news."

"I won't be able to come and visit you again."

"I understand," I respond, unsure what the correct answer is.

He throws his head up at the sky and laughs despite himself. "The fool that I am really thought I'd come to see you again and take you with me." He gathers my hands in his. "I forgot about all the good you do. When I got here, all I could think about was seeing you again, even if there was no chance you would leave all this and come with me."

"Martin —"

"And then I saw you here, relaxing on the stones, the sun bathing you in light I didn't know could still exist in this world. And that hope of you staying with me returned."

"You know I could never —"

"I know Adeline. I know. It's not a position I would ever want to put you in."

I suck in a deep breath. "Perhaps we could reunite once the war is over. We could see what a peaceful world has in store for us."

"You'll want to go back to America. I don't blame you for that, this continent is a mess and will be long after the treaties are signed. I couldn't ask you to stay after."

"Please don't make this an ultimatum. I have a duty to my girls, and to the patients. I have to see this through. I know there's more to our story, I truly believe that. I just don't see it going the way you're suggesting."

He suddenly becomes rigid, unmoving. "I'll write to you then."

"Please, don't be this way Martin."

"Farm in Lenexa, Kansas, right?

"Yes, but —"

"Then I'll write, and if the time is ever right for you, we'll see where it goes." Obviously disappointed in our grand reunion, he drops my hand and turns away. I'm left stunned to my spot. Scenes of our time together flash before my eyes like a film reel. After everything we've been through, every chance meeting and stolen kiss, I refuse to let it end this way.

I've never cared to run after a man before, but for whatever crazy reason, I run full speed after Martin. I catch him quickly, but he's in no mood to turn and talk to me, so I continue beside him, stride for stride. "I'm sorry if you think that this is just your decision to make, but it's mine too, so you better listen to me." He stops but doesn't look over. "If you leave me here like this today, then there's no reason for me to keep thinking about you when I shouldn't be. That's all I've done since the last time I saw you," I add. Finally, he looks over, daring to meet my gaze. "If you leave like this, it gives me my excuse to move on, and I don't want to move on yet. Not from you. I can't give you what you need now, but maybe someday I can. I want to."

His eyes search mine and his hand brushes the hair from my face. "I need to think."

I step back from him and nod.

Men always expect to get what they are demanding the moment that they ask for it. If I truly mean to him what he means to me, I'll still be a part of those demands months from now, if I'm lucky and God agrees, perhaps he'll still want me years from now.

Even as he walks away from me again, the flame inside of me grows stronger. Maybe it will dim for him in the next few months and we'll never speak again, but it's hard not to believe in a future for us. I knew the moment he opened his eyes on that gurney in France that our lives would be entwined, there's no way that this is the end of our story. As the wind picks up and blows my hair back into my face, I shut my eyes and affirm my belief that this is not the end of our story.

CHAPTER FORTY-EIGHT

Adeline

November 20, 1956
Barcelona, Spain

Martin opens the front door with one hand, the other guides me inside, steering me from my back. Our new home is bigger than anywhere I've ever lived, and the first house we've lived in as a family. The girls blow right by us into the empty entryway and then they disappear upstairs, undoubtedly heading to their rooms. Martin smiles as we step inside. With our furniture and belongings a few minutes behind us, the house is a shell waiting for us to make it a true home.

Martin and I had made a few trips to tour it while the girls stayed in France, so this is their first time seeing it in person. I'm glad they like it, as I know it was not easy for them to leave everything they knew in France. They loved it there, and because of their fondness, I too found love for it. With the way things have been in our little family since the disaster, I know we will make the best of things here together.

Still listening to the girls jumping around upstairs in their new rooms, Martin leans over and puts his hands on my stomach. The baby can't be more than the size of a peanut, we haven't even told the girls yet, but Martin has been speaking to it as if it's already in his arms. "Welcome home little one," he whispers.

I kiss Martin on the head and clutch his hand. We make our way through the house together, everything from the thick wooden shutters to the stucco arches between rooms is in order. I want nothing more than to plant flowers in the windowsills and hang up my girls' paintings, but for now, I will be content in holding my husband's hand as we watch our little girls bounce from room to room in awe.

When the trucks start to arrive with our belongings, I sweep the girls out the back door. Martin brings us a blanket and some of their toys to pass the time. He lays the blanket down in the grass, gives me a kiss, and then returns inside to direct the project of unloading. I settle onto the blanket, and the girls and I host a tea party for their dolls and animals.

The weather is nice here, warm and sunny even in the middle of fall. I find myself tilting my head up toward the sky so the sun can bathe me in its light. Our lives have been dreary for far too long, but here I feel like we can all start anew.

As the morning turns to afternoon, the movers take a break for lunch, allowing us time to go inside and see our home furnished. It's an odd combination to see our Spanish home adorned in the American style. Some might not like the look, but I for one think it represents our family perfectly.

We settle in for a quick lunch of sandwiches and fruit. The girls hurry through their meal, anxious to head up to their rooms and begin decorating. It's the first night they won't share a room, and I can only imagine what an ordeal it will be at bedtime.

Martin and I spend the rest of the lunch hour relaxing on the couch, still covered in its travel cloth. He props his feet up on a box, while I lay my head in his lap. He begins to run his fingers through my hair, but the band of his watch gets stuck.

"Sorry, darling," he says, untangling it. I expect the calming, brushing sensation to return, but when it doesn't, I tilt my head back to look up at him. "You know, we'll have to take this back in."

"Why?" Sitting back up, I take it from his hand to inspect it. "Is it broken already?"

"No, works like a charm. We'll just have to engrave another name on the back."

I smile and run my thumb over the cursive indented on the back. I return back to where I was laying before. Holding the watch close to my heart, I begin to think about New York and Eloisa. Martin returns his hands to the waves in my hair.

"I want to send Eloisa a letter tonight while we're out. I haven't sent one in a while, and I'd like her to have our new address."

"Of course," he replies. "I hope she is getting along all right."

I sigh. "She wrote that she was going to the hearings."

"Alone?"

"Yes."

"It's dumbfounding to me that they didn't go through with the proceedings. After everything that happened, there needs to be someone held accountable."

Eloisa had made it clear to me in her most recent letter that she didn't blame anyone for what happened, it was an accident that was the outcome of a series of unfortunate events. Even with this sentiment, I still want to fight for her, for all of them. An out-of-court settlement was reached earlier this month, and the hearings were ended without notice. I can't imagine what Eloisa, or even Arden, went through when they heard the news. Such a taxing, emotional chapter slammed shut without any sort of warning.

"I just don't want people to forget about them. Forget about the collision, fine, but the victims? They have to be remembered."

"I'm sure they will, love." While Martin doesn't seem nearly as worried as I do, I know he cares deep down. I know he cares about Eloisa, as he asks about her often.

A knock on the door signals the return of the movers. Martin kisses the back of my hand before heading to the front door. I sit up slowly, trying to stave off the rush of dizziness. As the men swarm, I force myself off the velvet settee and go on a search for my daughters. On the way upstairs, I take Martin's watch and clasp it on my wrist. Even on its tightest fit, it still hangs loose on me. Like most of his things, they don't quite feel right, but I'm happy to wear them just to feel him close.

I find them in Juliet's room laying on their stomachs and reading a book together. They're both bent at the knee, legs crossed at the ankles. I watch them for a moment from the door. Precious moments like this are what motherhood means to me. It's easy to get caught up in the rush of day-to-day life, but when you slow down and take in a scene like this, it can be the most serene and tranquil moment of the day.

Johanna catches me out of the corner of her eye and then jumps up. "Maman, you must look at how I've decorated my room!"

She takes my hand and we cross the hallway, Juliet following close behind. Sure enough, the room is already sparkling with Johanna's style. Everything is nice and neat, books are already on her shelves, her bed is already made ... I didn't even know the linens had made it inside yet. She is the opposite of her sister who is all clutter and comfort. Watching them find their own identities, their own personalities, has been an honor.

The rest of the afternoon is spent making the house functional for the night. The girls help in every way they can until they get bored. Martin does the heavy lifting, while I give the instructions. I put on the Buddy Holly record I smuggled from New York to fill the work time with singing and dancing.

When it's all said and done, and we've done enough organization to make a receptionist go crazy, we call it a day. The sun is just beginning to dip below our new horizon as we exit our house and walk down the street. With each of us holding a twin, Martin and I are able to hold hands as we take a stroll down our block. The neighborhood is alive; people tend to their gardens, while others walk toward the city center. Live music pours from cafés and restaurants. The culture isn't nearly as different as I thought it would be. Enveloped in the warm colors of sunset, I lean over and wrap my free arm around Martin's. I want to freeze this moment the way it is, the four of us exploring our new world together, happy and perfectly content.

CHAPTER FORTY-NINE

Arden

December 13, 1939
Gothenburg, Sweden

Nora is my St. Lucia. Her face is lit by the soft glow of the candles stacked upon her wreathed head, tranquil in prayer, an angel with hair braided into buns. As the church bursts into the final chorus of "Sankta Lucia", I avert my attention to the front where the children sing and our congregation's chosen young Lucia stands regally, honored to have been given the opportunity. A tradition for centuries, we celebrate the feast of St. Lucia.

When the final echo has dissipated, the crowd gathers their things and migrates to the streets. The great feast is still to be had. Outside the longest table you could ever imagine sits in the street covering an entire block. People emerge from their homes with food and set the table. Girls extinguish their candle crowns and pull up their white robes so as not to muddy them with the wintry mix of old snow and new.

I do the honor for my lovely wife. Blowing out each candle carefully, I pluck the crown from her head, her flaxen blonde hair tumbles onto her shoulders, half braided. Embarrassed, she curls in on herself, hugging her swollen belly. It's something she does when she's beautiful and knows it but doesn't want to admit it. I have to rub the astonishment from my face before reaching out to unfurl her. I hold my hand against her stomach and think about how next year we will be celebrating with a little one.

The feast is lively, people sing and dance, and the food is filling. With so much tension in the world, it's heartening to know that joy can still be had. Nora eats, and when she's finished, I encourage her to eat some off my plate. It takes some coaxing before she does, knowing she'll lose the battle no matter what. She's mourning the fact that this is the first Christmas season she is away from her family in Hässleholm. As a light snow begins to fall, I wrap an arm around her to stave off the cold and the isolating emotions.

I would do anything to make her happy. I would give her the world if I could, but I'm afraid all I've been able to offer her since we were wed is my love and protection. I hope they will not be the only things I can promise her in our life together, but if not, I know they will be enough to keep us together. I love her, she loves me, and I will not let anything happen to her, that is all that matters to me.

Throughout the meal, we are blessed and prayed over by neighbors and strangers alike. Everyone wants to know the name of the baby, but the truth is we haven't chosen one. Nora is the most free-spirited, albeit shy, woman I've ever met, which means she is not one to make traditional decisions. She claims the name will come to her when she sees the babe for the first time. Who am I to challenge a mother's intuition? I am no one compared to her. Even now, as she leans back to relieve some of the pressure on her back, she is steeped in the warm flames, and she is the most beautiful thing I've ever seen. She holds out her hand to me and I take it. Our attention turns to the performers as the air shifts, the sudden breeze throwing skirts and tapestries billowing into it, demanding the attention of those gathered.

A guitar and violin start to play a somber tune, a song everyone will know. Nora grips my hand tighter as the woman's haunting voice floats through the crowd to the table where we watch. A shiver runs through me as "*Så Rider Jag Mig*" is played.

An old folk song about a young woman dying, and how her lover can't bring himself to go on living as he did before.

> "*Jag krusar och kammar mitt fagergula
> har,*" they sing.
> I curl and comb my fair-yellow hair.

"Och ville följa henne till graven."
And wanted to follow her to the grave.
"De sa jag skull' få välja ut en annan."
They said that I would choose another.
"En sådan en flicka såson hon var."
Such a girl she was.
"Finns ej i sju konungariken."
She doesn't exist anywhere else in the
seven kingdoms.

Nora reaches over and wipes the tears that I didn't know I was crying. "We should go," she whispers. I can tell she's concerned about me, so I pull myself together and drape my overcoat around her shoulders.

Even as we leave the gathering behind, the singer's words reverberate through my brain. The woman beside me holds strong as we make our way through the snow-dusted streets to our one room home. I'll keep the fire burning tonight so she can get a good night's sleep, and tomorrow I will continue to search for a job that doesn't lead to a dead end. We have enough money to line our pocket, but the deeper we get into winter, the more expensive things become.

"If I asked you to carry me home, would you?" Nora asks with a laugh.

"You don't have to ask," I say, already moving to scoop her up.

With the eerie song left behind, I focus on putting my feet right on the slippery path before me. We're only a block away, I could carry her across the world if she needed me to. When we reach the front door, I let her down and she moves to unlock it, but I stop her before she can. Turning back to the street, I hold her tightly against me, afraid to let her go. She rests her head against my upper arm, it's all the height she has, and then she guides my free hand to her stomach.

"I think it's a girl," she says in a hushed voice, as if she isn't sure she wanted me to hear her.

Who am I to challenge a woman's intuition? "I think so too."

We're silent as we look out into the darkened neighborhood. Most of the city is still alive with celebrations, but our street is calm, not a light to be seen. It seems the world has left us alone, even if just for a moment.

"Nora?" She tilts her head up, her eyes dancing with an ember glow. "You know there is nothing I wouldn't do for you?"

She doesn't draw away, doesn't squirm. She answers me with the confidence of a warrior. "I wouldn't have married you if I thought differently. I hope you chose me because you felt the same."

She reaches up and presses her palm to my cheek. "It is us." She pauses to emphasize her stomach. "It is us, and soon this child. That is all that matters, now and forever."

"Until the next one?" I say, looking deeply into her eyes, imagining six children with her eyes.

"Until the next one."

We can't be sure how many we will be blessed with in the future, but one thing is for certain: I will love and protect them all as long as I live.

CHAPTER FIFTY

Arden

December 13, 1956
MS Stockholm, the Atlantic Ocean

The sea wraps its welcoming arms around me as the Stockholm's new bow slices through the ice-ridden water. As the storm clouds that have hung over me since the collision start to clear, I am finally able to breathe again. The freezing winter air is full of new opportunities, and I am finally going home. At this time tomorrow, I will be face to face with my past. My heart pace quickens at the thought of it being so close, but when the ring on my hand clinks against the handrail of the bow, I am reminded of all it took to get here. I stare down at the gold band glistening in the dying sun before looking out to the horizon. Every step I took away from my life in London was a step toward a new forever. I don't know where it will lead me yet, but I do know that sometime tonight the shores of Sweden will be visible from where I stand. For the first time, I will be able to look at it without dread or fear of what it holds for me.

Nearly 4,000 miles behind me is a young girl who has just started her journey into healing from loss. Eloisa, the girl who gave me the chance to start again, the girl who helped to remind me that self-forgiveness is always possible. Before I met her, my days were plagued with loneliness. There is no doubt that my life will always be lonely, and no one will ever replace my girls, but for the first time the voices in my head attempting to fill the void are not ghosts, they are alive.

"Lund?"

With it being so cold, I'm surprised to hear my name. Turning, I find Dawe approaching. He is bundled up, his wool coat collar pulled as far up his neck as he can, and a condensation cloud leaves his lips every time he breathes. I nod as he steps up to the rail beside me. He knocks it with his fist and stomps the wooden deck with his boots.

"I never thought I'd sail on an American-built ship," he says.

"Neither did I."

"I've been wondering how much she has left in her." His fists soften, and he rests his palm on the rail, leaning into it.

"There's life to her yet. I still think she'll outlive me."

"Oh, you don't mean that."

"You know my friend, I think that I do. I can feel it in my bones."

"With the way the world is these days, the Andrea Doria is better off at the bottom of the ocean." He lights a cigarette, and there is no apology in his voice. Of course, I know what he means. We are all a dying breed out here, ships and crew alike. As the days go by, people take to the air, and more and more good ships get sold for scrap. The Andrea Doria will last longer at the bottom of the ocean than she would up here with the rest of us.

"Can I ask you something, Dawe?"

He grips my shoulder. "Arden, today you can ask me just about anything."

"Do you think it was our fault?"

"I think it was God's plan," he shrugs, as if I'm dumb for not having thought of it already. "People live and people die. Disasters happen and we move on. I would have thought you knew that better than anyone."

"I do, but I don't think the survivors would care to think of the same sentiment after losing so much."

"Are you thinking about Eloisa?"

I nod. "Of course, how can I not."

"You think of her as a daughter?" he asks.

"I do. I know it might be hard to understand."

I realize I have never asked about his family. "Do you have children?"

"I had a daughter." He doesn't elaborate, and I don't ask him to.

As stars become visible and night falls, the ship reduces its speed. As Dawe takes a look up at the brilliant open sky, he taps the side of the rail and sticks out a hand toward me. I think we both know this could be the last time we see each other, so a handshake in lieu of a salute suits me just fine.

"Sure you don't want to come in? They're putting on a little celebration for Saint Lucy's Day," Dawe says, looking once more at the stars. My heart drops at the mention of the holiday.

I can't bring myself to smile as I answer him. "I haven't celebrated since before the war."

Dawe studies me for a moment, but ultimately leaves it be. "All right, well at least stay warm, it's going to be the coldest night of the voyage."

As Dawe disappears in the warm glow of the interior salon to mingle with passengers, I look back out to the dark water. If I've learned anything in my time traveling, it's the fact the sea does not discriminate. Young, bright, fair, it doesn't matter. Whatever you have going for you, or against you, it can all be taken in a moment. It's a wonder to me that I've never felt trapped by this beast of judge, jury, and executioner, at least until now. For the first time in my life, the sea is what is trapping me, not the faults of my past.

With the temperature continuing to drop, I pop my collar and push my hands deeper into my pockets where an opened letter rests. I curl my fingers around it and hold on for dear life. A letter from Nora's parents arrived a few days before I left. I collapsed in tears when I read its contents. Knowing everything will be okay, I take a deep breath and squint my eyes toward the horizon, anxious to see land, desperate to see Sweden. For I know that when I do, I will finally be free of everything that has pinned me for so long.

CHAPTER FIFTY-ONE

Eloisa

July 10, 1945
Bari, Italy

The beaches have been cleared of their defenses, and the water has finally lost all signs of the oil and blood that afflicted it throughout the last five years. It is hot outside, people are laughing, and the war is over. Among those people enjoying the heat are Anita, Dino, Leo, and I.

Together we flock down the seaside promenade toward the Polignano a Mare beach. The sandy spot named after bread and tomatoes holds a special place in me. It's where my parents first met, and where they would take me every summer day until the war came. Papà is far too busy with work to visit, and Mamma is extra peculiar with how she keeps the apartment these days. I've been left to share the beach with the friends the war thrust upon me.

As the ground beneath our feet changes from concrete to sand, Dino reaches out for Anita's hand. Leo and I watch from behind them as she swats it away but then quickly gives in. I see the shy look they give each other as they head to the shore, fingers intertwined.

"May I hold yours?" Leo asks beside me.

Feeling honored that he would ask, I don't answer him. Instead, I'm the one to make the move. He smiles at me in his sweet way, and we swing our arms back and forth like they do in the movies. It feels as though we can take on the whole world. We've survived a war that found its way into our home, to the streets of our beloved Bari. If we can survive that, then we can survive anything.

When we reach the shore, I wiggle my toes in the water freely for the first time in years. Even in such a crowded spot, the four of us are able to share this monumental occasion of freedom. Children when all of this started, we're young teens now dealing with the fallout. In due time things will return to normal, or as normal as they can be, just like the water in front of us. Just as the war lives within me, it also lives within the ocean. While the visuals are gone, such as the oil in the water or the cuts on my feet from the never-ending broken glass, just as the ships sit beneath the waves in the harbor, the scars on my feet will forever be there.

I've never been afraid of the ocean, but today I can't bring myself to go past my knees. I scrunch up my skirt in the front, but the back side is skimming the waves. The line where the sky meets the sea now represents the unknown to me, while it once used to stir a grand sense of discovery. I'd hate to lose my love for adventure, but with such a big violent world out there, I don't know if it's worth it. Bari represents safety and home, the place I weathered the biggest storm of my life. Why so many other people are discussing leaving baffles me.

Despite my long staring contest with the horizon, Leo still holds tight to my hand, seemingly taking in the same sensations as I am. Even when I glance at him from the corner of my eye, I can see how beautiful he is, inside and out. I wrap my arms around him and breathe him in. Draping an arm across my back, he holds me close to him and rests his lips on my head. It's not a kiss but more a sign of warning to those around, or a sign of protection. I'm so lucky to have someone so gentle, someone so in tune with my feelings.

Leo doesn't push me when I refuse to go out further into the water with him, even though he wants me to. Instead, we wade back to the shore and sit in the sand next to our discarded shoes. I watch Dino and Anita swim while Leo traces the lines on my palm.

"Are you all right Eloisa?" he asks.

"I've just been thinking about everything we've gone through here, about all the people leaving Bari behind."

He stops tracing my hand. "It's different now."

"Of course it is," I whisper. "How could it not be?"

Leo overturns my hand and sets it against his thigh. "There's more to life than Bari. I think a lot of people have started to realize that they don't want to spend their whole life here." He looks at me with hurt in his eyes. I straighten up with realization.

"Is that what you think too?"

"I —"

"Hey, love birds!" Anita calls. I drag my eyes away from Leo to my soaking-wet friend who's wrapping a towel around her shoulders. She drops to the ground next to us, and Dino joins us shortly with a few glass bottles full of American soda.

Leo gently kisses the back of my hand and gives me a look that implies we'll finish the conversation when we're alone. I look back out to the shore, trying to see what he sees, trying to imagine a forever with him out there.

My family's little flat on the second floor used to be my happy place, but now it tends to be full of long silences and sad songs on the radio. Sitting down for dinner across from my father, he doesn't acknowledge me, while my mother cuts her chicken in silence. I look down at my food and think of all the times we were happy sitting here eating together.

I wish I could do more to make Papà happy, but Mamma says he won't ever be the same. She had called me a grown-up when she told me what he suffers from, that I had to see the situation through the tired eyes of someone her age. It's hard for me to understand why someone could be so sad all the time. He still walks with a bad limp from the night the Nazis bombed the harbor, but he has two girls who love him more than anything. I don't understand what more he needs. I often try to tell myself that having my parents is enough, that it will always be enough.

Someday we'll be happy again.

The night I cowered in the cupboard with Leo, I thought I had lost them. A chill runs through me when I remember the feelings of that night. It's not a feeling I can ever forget. I fear that the moment I do is the moment I forget I need them.

I set my knife and fork down on the table and scrounge up the courage to speak. "Mamma, Papà, I love you,"

I watch as his face softens. "I love you too, Eloisa."

Mamma reaches across the table and rests her hand on my wrist. "I love you, my dear girl."

Nothing more is said during the meal. Of course, I wanted to tell my parents about the beach, and how it's returned to its formal beauty, but I don't. They still love me, that's all that matters, and that's all I needed to know. They will want to talk again in time, just like the birds would after an air raid.

After I've cleared the table, my father stops me on my way to my room. Nothing is said as he struggles to bend down on his injured leg. When he's at eye level with me, he pulls me into a bone-crushing hug. It sends me back to when we found him after the bombing. The smoky smell of that day is replaced by my father's cologne and the lingering scent of dinner. My mother watches, tears welling in her eyes, a damp dishtowel still hanging from her right hand.

Someday they'll be happy again.

I can't be sure, but as he pulls away, I swear he wipes away tears in his eyes. I kiss him on the cheek and move past him and into my room where I can disappear into whatever reality I want. Pulling my newest sketchbook from the shelf by the window, I draw every detail of today. Someday, when Papà is ready to talk again, I'll be able to tell him about all the days he missed. This thought bolsters me to keep drawing well into the night until my fingers are cramped and sore.

Someday I'll be happy again.

CHAPTER FIFTY-TWO

Eloisa

July 25, 2006
The Atlantic Ocean

As Gino escorts me from my small upper deck cabin to the main deck, I take joy in the sun shining through the clouds. It was not an easy journey to get here last night, and I'm afraid my stomach isn't what it once was.

Gino and I join the group of aging survivors who have become good friends throughout the years. Many of us have been coming to the reunions since the beginning, since we were still kids it seems like. This year is the 50th anniversary of the sinking, and while some wounds never heal, it has been therapeutic for me. For three days out of the year, I allow myself to go back to the hardest months of my life. It helps me compartmentalize the whole thing, to put the pain away all other 362 days.

This year has been especially heavy as the ship continues to take its toll. Not a week ago a diver lost his life, becoming the eleventh to do so. They call the wreck the Mount Everest of diving because of its treacherous depth and the treasures it holds.

I have become friends with many researchers and divers throughout the years, as I have become known to those interested, as 'the girl who liked art'. Many of the pieces I looked at with Leo on our excursion day have been returned to the surface, including the Guido Gambone panels, which I have had the pleasure to see again many times during our yearly receptions.

While many gathered here have brought their families to witness the commemoration this year, my own decided to stay on land. They argued that this day is for my brother and I, and that they don't want me to hold back my emotions on account of them being there. It was very honorable of them to do this. I've seen ill-behaving relatives hog the spotlight or presume to know what it was like to be there that night. Perhaps that's just me in my old lady way of thinking, but I'm relieved that my family would rather not even be tempted to act in such a way.

The only family member that matters to me today is Gino. Too young to remember anything, he visits to feel closer to our parents and Lucia, to talk to them and remember them. We often hang back from the crowd and the media crews so that we can have our moment without interference.

As the ship circles the spot where the Andrea Doria now sits nearly 200 feet below the surface, Gino and

I approach the stern. When the engines stop the ceremony begins. Prayers are said and flowers are thrown over the side of the ship.

Though I haven't cried here in decades, today is different. When the media starts their segments, Gino and I slip away to midship. Marking where the collision happened, we link hands and begin our prayers. Today, I let the emotions flow freely. Gino notices and breaks his prayer to try and bolster me. I shake him away. We both know this is likely my last trip out here, so I'm willing to feel the brevity of the moment.

The first gift in our growing pile is for Marjorie and Jack Baker. Their children, Joanie and Jonah, never came back to New York City after their mother passed away in the 80s. Family friends since the day I met them, Gino and I make sure to drop wreaths for them every year.

Next, we toss a wreath over for Mamma and Papà. Gino tries to play up his emotions for me, but I know he will never know them the way that I did, and that's okay.

Bundled sunflowers go in next for our sister. My darling Lucia, whom I never forgave myself for leaving alone. I know for a fact she had never seen a sunflower in her life, but when I first saw one in full bloom looking up at the sun, I cried for an hour because to me that was my sister in flower form. Ever since then, they have come with me everywhere.

I cannot bring myself to pick up the final two gifts in the pile at my feet.

"Gino?" I ask.

"Yes, Eloisa?" My brother rests a hand on my back, ever the comfort.

"May I be left alone for this part?"

He holds my face in his hands and nods. "You must tell Arden that I miss hearing from him." He kisses me on both cheeks before turning away. He moves several sections down where he will continue his praying and daydreaming of what could have been.

In this spot fifty years ago, I was torn apart from the love of my life. Without him, I have made a life for myself. I have a husband who loves me, children I wouldn't trade for the world, and grandchildren who love to hear stories about my childhood ... but still, I can't help but imagine a life with my first love. I know I shouldn't, and I could never admit it out loud, but it's my truth.

"It heartens me to know that I will be seeing you soon, my love." I toss one singular flower in, not ready to let go of the whole wreath.

When the doctor told me I had cancer, I did not weep. I realized how happy it made me to think about seeing my parents, sister, and Leo again. Of course, there's not much to be done for me anyway, it's been manifesting inside me since December 2, 1943.

I told Leo the truth of that night in my prayers when the details came to light in 1967. I thought I had been spared the worst of it, but it turns out that wasn't the case. The odd smell that covered everything, from the air I breathed to the clothes on my father's back, wasn't garlic but mustard gas. Dino died from it years ago, and Anita followed soon after. Thousands in Bari are afflicted by it.

I want to be with them again so badly it hurts. Perhaps it makes me a bad Christian to want to move on from this earth. But is it wrong to love someone so much even in death that you want to see them again? I know it will hurt those that love me, but deep down they know I share my love with another family. My husband knows I share my love with another man.

"I've been so patient, Leo. I know you have too. Just know that I'm coming to see you soon."

Holding up the wreath with his name written in big cursive letters on the card, I toss it over the side where it joins a field of others. I close my eyes and breathe in the ocean spray; it takes me back to the deck of the Andrea Doria where my family walked together happily for the last time. It's the memory I tend to go back to the most. Of course, there are days I wish I could go back and change things, but with that being impossible, I do my best to remember the best moments.

Saying a silent prayer for their souls and my own, I reach to my feet where the last bouquet sits with little gifts tucked inside. I hold it out over the rail, but I can't let it go quite yet. I study the letters plastered to the stems. There are three, Gino's, Adeline, and mine. All are addressed to Arden wherever he may be.

When Arden left for Sweden after the collision, I knew I would never see him again, and still, I wept when I heard he had died. A mysterious package from Sweden had arrived in my mailbox. Arden and I conversed regularly, and Adeline too, but he never sent me packages. When I opened it, I found a letter and a few of his belongings. The letter explained that Arden had passed away from a heart attack. One of his cousins had found my old letters in the drawer by his bedside and made sure to send me the news and his things, including his watch and a picture of him aboard the Stockholm, his beloved ship that still sails the ocean as a passenger ship. His watch and photo now sit on my mantle for all to see and inquire about.

When I wrote to Adeline about it, she too seemed saddened by it. I know they knew each other for only a few weeks, but the bond the three of us built in our loneliest days after the disaster was strong, and still is. Though Adeline is now confined to living in her family home in Spain with Juliet and her family, she still makes the time to write to me. I never did make good on the promise to visit her there, but I know she understands. She continues to send gifts in the weeks before the anniversary for me to send out to sea for Arden and my family. Her notes are always labeled in her flowing cursive, though it has become shakier in the past few years. I've never read what she's written out of respect for her and the dead, but I'm sure it's something Arden loves seeing year after year.

I take a whiff of the roses and then hold them out over the ledge once again. "Arden my old friend, I miss hearing of your adventures." I let the collection tip out of my hands. They land right-side up in the water and are immediately carried by the current away from the vessel. Craning my neck back behind me, I wave my brother away from the wall he stands against. He unclasps his folded hands and moves to join me.

Though he doesn't remember anything from the sinking, he has heard the stories hundreds of times from me. He also has sketches of Mamma, Papà, and Lucia I drew framed in his home. It pains me to know his view of them was shaped only by my drawings and descriptions. There are no photos of them to speak of. Those that do exist are laying in a tomb at the bottom of the ocean.

Gino and I face each other and link hands. Gino leads a lengthy prayer, and by the end he has attracted a dozen or so people. When the final amen is spoken, we cross ourselves and the crowd breaks off.

The ship sounds three sharp blasts on its whistle before turning and heading back to land. I wander to the bow and look out beyond. The next time I step foot on land will be the last time I do so on this earth. Looking up at the sky, I know I'm bound for one more stop. I will join all those that I've loved once more, where they reside on the shore of forever.

The End

AUTHOR'S NOTE

This novel was years in the making. Honestly, my love for this pinpoint in history dates back to when I was handed my first book about shipwrecks in kindergarten. I have been overly fascinated by them ever since.

Being historically accurate is very important to me, and while I don't think it's possible to be perfectly accurate when it comes to historical fiction, I did take it very seriously when creating this novel. Unlike other historical ships like the Titanic, where every inch of the ship is known and every detail of the wreck uncovered, there is still a lot of unknown when it comes to the Andrea Doria, Stockholm, and Île de France. I was as thorough as I could be, but I left it up to my imagination to fill in the gaps when necessary.

Not only did I have to do research on three different ships, I also had to do research on three different countries during WWII. The attack on Bari, Italy, was something I stumbled upon while researching, and I was surprised I hadn't heard about it before. That's the best part about being a historical writer in my opinion, that the process allows me to learn more about a topic than I ever intended to.

I truly hope this book inspires readers to do more research for themselves. I tried to squeeze in as much fascinating detail as I could, but history is infinitely vast, so there is always more to learn.

Although Eloisa, Arden, and Adeline are fictional characters, they were inspired by countless stories I read about real people at the time. It was an era in history when the world was trying to find a new identity after the war. There was a large shift in immigration, and different countries throughout the world were trying their best to overcome what they had endured. My main characters are derived from this idea of the world reborn in the 1950s.

For more information about this tragedy and others like it, I would recommend reading, *The Last Voyage of the Andrea Doria: The Sinking of the World's Most Glamorous Ship* by Greg King and Penny Wilson. YouTube channels: *Oceanliner Designs, Bright Sun Films,* and *Casual Navigation* also have excellent videos that discuss the sinking and transatlantic travel during the 1950s.

ACKNOWLEGEMENTS

Where do I even start? So many people have backed me on my journey to make this dream of publishing a reality. Friends, family, and complete strangers have shown their support via social media and, of course, a wild Kickstarter campaign.

To my incredible fiancé, who will be my husband shortly after the time this is published, I love you so much and hope you hear me when I say that I could not have done this without your love and support.

To those in my family that encouraged me to learn about history growing up and in turn told me to chase this dream of becoming an author. Thank you for putting so much of your energy and time into me.

To a few incredible educators I have had over the years, I want to thank you for instilling a belief in me that I am a good writer, and that my talent shouldn't be wasted. Thank you for coaching me to be the best critical thinker that I can be when it comes to developing written work. I would be nowhere without you all!

To my amazing editor and designer, you ladies helped this novel reach its fullest potential, and I am so honored to have worked with you.

To Amy Harmon, Noelle Salazar, Julie Olivia, and Ruta Sepetys, thank you for answering all of my questions when it came to writing and publishing. I wish I had the words to tell you how much your books mean to me.

To all my wonderful Kickstarter supporters, you are seriously so incredible for taking a chance on this project. I hope it exceeded your expectations. My head is forever spinning about the fact that you accomplished what you did.

I have to especially call out Jared Kimbrough, Craig Moore, Marc Maxwell, Lance Maxwell, Kevin Chapman, Laine Chapman, Derek Greenamoyer, Lynda Rutkowski, Matt Steward, and Paul Thompson! Thank you all for your generous donations, I hope the book made you proud!

Finally, to those that are reading this, whomever you may be, I am incredibly thankful to you for taking the time to read this novel of mine. I hope it inspired you, moved you, or helped you disappear to another time for a few hours.

Until the next adventure,

Elora

ABOUT THE AUTHOR

Elora Maxwell is an independent historical fiction author. She writes historical things, romantic things, fantastical things, and sometimes devastatingly sad things. When she's not traveling through time, she likes visiting amusement parks, watching movies, and forcing everyone around her to listen to Taylor Swift.

Instagram: @author_eloramaxwell
TikTok: @author_eloramaxwell

Made in the USA
Las Vegas, NV
29 February 2024